BONNIE SYNCLAIRE

CRASH AND BURN

FBI: Criminal Profilers #1

PITTSBURGH

This is a work of fiction. Names, characters, places, and events are the products of the author's imagination and any resemblance to actual events or places or persons, living or dead, is entirely coincidental.

ISBN (trade paperback): 9798330551347 | ISBN (ebook): 9798223255208
Published by Sinclair Publishing LLC
Distributed by IngramSpark
POD | Printed in the USA

Version 1, December 2023

Cover images credits: man - Andre Hunter/Unsplash; woman - StockSnap; smokey background - Camille Couvez/Unsplash

BOOKS BY BONNIE SYNCLAIRE

Rogue

Incognito

Promises We Break

Crash And Burn

Line of Fire

AUTHOR'S NOTE

The FBI's Violent Crimes Division is real. However, I created my own fictional team—the Criminal Profiling Unit—that works within the VCU for the sake of the story.

~ B.S.

DEDICATION

For my grandmother, Bonnie Faye. Every story I pen is dedicated to you.

And in loving memory of my uncle, Rupert West. A fellow writer, editor, and a staple in the Black literary industry, your legacy continues to inspire me as a novelist.

~ B.S.

PART ONE

PROLOGUE

1 Year Before

THE ROOM SEEMED TO SWAY beneath her feet, even though she was sitting down. She gripped the arms of her chair as the edges of her vision darkened and everything began to blur, and all the noise in the room faded. It felt as if she was being transported back to that fateful night—a night she never thought she would have to relive again. She couldn't stop her mind from taking her back...

It was raining. No, pouring. It was the kind of rain that came down in large merciless drops, blurring the world around you, stinging your eyes and burning your skin. Roaring thunder from the storm raged loudly outside of the windowpane, making the inside of the building appear darker than it usually was in the night.

She was running, trying unsuccessfully to find an escape somewhere in the darkness. She stopped to catch her breath, her body shaking after the end of a sudden rush of adrenaline, her heart beating in her ears, and she turned around to see a tall, menacing shadow emerge and move slowly down the hall, coming toward her. It was too dark to see much of anything, but she knew that he was after her. She also knew that she probably looked like a wreck; her clothes were wrinkled, her perfect ballet bun now messied and uneven, the dark red blood stains on her shirt showing obvious signs of being in a struggle.

She tried to load the last bullet she had with clammy hands into the long, skinny gun her father had given to her that she didn't know the name of, but she forgot a step. She fumbled with the gun as she walked backward down the empty corridor, mentally racking her brain to remember how to load it. A few moments later it made a faint clicking sound, the two pieces snapping together into place. Yes! The figure was creeping closer, but she was ready now. Slowing down her breathing and doing her best to control the new wave of adrenaline that coursed through her body, she aimed directly in front of her and squinted into the dimness.

She waited another moment, then pulled the trigger...
She missed.

The distress of having missed the shot jolted her back into where she was now, back into the present and reality.

The memory had faded just as quickly as it came, and everything reappeared. Neevah Alistair-Winters looked around the small, outdated conference room to see that everyone was still listening to the producer's ramblings. No one realized that she was no longer paying attention to what he was saying. She shifted in her chair to sit up straighter and rubbed her now sweaty palms along her pants, being sure to maintain her poise.

"...Just think about it." Barry Hayes, an openly money-hungry film producer from a state that was far from Pennsylvania, pressed his stubby pointer finger down into the glass table, emphasizing whatever point he was trying to make. "This is what the people want. True crime and documentary ratings have both skyrocketed over the last decade, and this is the time to tell your family's story the way you want it: unedited, unfiltered, real. This can be huge for everyone involved. You guys wanted this case reopened, right? With this kind of spotlight on the city, they won't make the mistake of ignoring you this time. And Neevah, I have to say it, we've all seen the rave reviews on your books. You're the hottest true crime writer out there; the people can't get enough of the stories you're helping shed a light on. Now is your time to be heard. The world wants to know your story..."

When Neevah didn't respond, her husband Owen Winters placed a gentle hand on her leg, showing his support. She drew in a deep breath. "But...what about my sister, and my parents? What do they have to say about this?"

Barry Hayes leaned forward in his seat. "Actually, everybody's already on board." he said with a grin. "We're just waiting for you."

• • •

Present Day

Neevah's hand shook as she lifted the styrofoam cup to her lips and took a long sip of the steaming hot espresso. She needed to pull herself together; no one else was trembling like she was, and she mentally kicked herself for looking so weak. She had agreed to do this, and now she had to go through with it.

"Take five, everyone." Hayes announced, and Neevah hurriedly snatched up her car keys, grabbed her peacoat, and exited the production studio before anyone would realize that she'd left. She made a few short strides over to her car, a late-model silver Porsche 718 Boxster, and gratefully climbed in and closed the door, embracing her own personal space.

She gulped down the rest of her coffee and dialed her husband's phone number. After one ring, he picked up.

"Is everything alright?" he said. Owen Winters was a journalist with a highly impressive career in not only reporting on unraveling criminal investigations, jury trials, arrests, and breaking news, but also reporting stories that dealt with crime, politics, and civil unrest within their city. His career was almost as exciting as his wife's; Neevah was a highly accoladed and bestselling true crime novelist, making a living writing about other people's nightmares and traveling across the globe, sometimes even visiting her clients one-on-one to hear their stories in person and turn them into books, attending exclusive writers' conferences, award ceremonies, and speaking engagements. They were both highly passionate about their work and supported each other in everything they did.

"Yeah, everything's fine. We're just taking a break." Neevah didn't feel like talking that much, she just wanted to hear him talk instead. "How's your first day back on the job?"

"Honestly? It feels like I never left." Owen replied. Just four months ago, he'd decided to take time off of work to travel alongside Neevah for her latest worldwide book tour, and this was their first week back at home. Everything already felt so foreign even though they had both spent most of their adult lives in Ruxlor City. "Everything is go-go-go as usual, but I like it. And I got a couple of interns from the community college that I'm going to mentor as well."

"That's great, honey…" Her voice drifted off as she peered past the parking lot and into the wooded area beyond it. She could have swore she saw something out of the corner of her eye, but she dismissed it.

"Are you sure you're okay?"

Neevah shook her head. I'm probably just seeing things. Being paranoid. "Me? Of course, yeah. Just tired, is all. I'll see you at home."

"Great. I'll have dinner waiting."

They said their goodbyes, and Neevah pocketed her cell phone. She took a deep breath, mentally preparing herself to walk back into the studio. She exited her car and looked around the parking lot, but the only person there was her. She sighed and made her way back inside.

Whatever she thought she'd seen, it was gone.

• • •

The figure was crouched behind the dying bush in the thick woodlands, studying Neevah as she got out of her car and walked back into the studio, hugging her arms around herself to brace against the bitter cold. He could easily tell by her body language that she was tired, frazzled, and clearly uncomfortable.

She had the right to be. If only she knew what was to come. *They should have left it all alone.*

He jotted down her license plate number in a small, worn leather notepad, gathered up his supplies, and stood. He turned and began his trek back through the woods, headed for the ever-bustling city.

1

HE SMELLED THE AWFUL SCENT of singed wood before he saw it.

Officer Hunter's face twisted up and he glanced over at his partner. "What is that?"

"Don't know..." Officer Williams, Hunter's usual night shift patrol partner, shifted in the passenger seat and squinted around. She pointed out of the open window into the distance. "Looks like something down Mills Run Road. We should check it out."

Flynn obliged, turning the police cruiser down the dark road. It mainly consisted of older and outdated commercial properties, some that hadn't been occupied in years, others still fairly successful. The street lights had died long ago, and the only thing that illuminated the road were the headlights from the car.

And an orange glow in the distance.

Neither officer said anything as they ventured down the road in silence. As they crept closer to the source of the glow, they quickly realized that it was a fire. And it was spreading. Fast.

Hunter parked on the side of the road just a few yards away and quickly retrieved his walkie-talkie, watching thin trails of smoke come from the windows. "Dispatch, this is twenty-four." he spoke into it.

"Got something, Hunter?" Eve, the overnight dispatcher, responded.

"We got a building fire on Mills Run Road, right by—"

"—Wait, someone's in there." Officer Williams said to Officer Hunter, and she scrambled to get out of the car.

"Williams, wait for..." Hunter started, but she had already gotten out and closed the passenger side door, leaving him behind.

She could hear a voice coming from the burning building. It sounded like a male voice, a distressed one, at that. Whoever he was, he was screaming out in agony, pleading for help. The air was permeated gray and growing thicker by now, causing her eyes to water and to cough lightly, but that didn't stop the young officer from walking closer to the fire, trying to locate the unfortunate person.

There, the oxygen escaped the officer's lungs as her eyes fell upon the source of the screams: a man sat tied to a chair inside, duct tape strapped across his mouth, burning alive.

2

IT WAS AN UNUSUALLY BRIGHT and sunny October afternoon when Jonah Davenport visited the memorial grounds with his father, Senior Detective Samuel Davenport.

Jonah walked down the invisible trail he knew by heart, passing large stones crafted from glistening granite and marble, and stopped at a smaller and more simpler memorial: a small white quartz rectangle with flying doves in each corner. He knelt down on one knee, pushed away the brown, orange, and yellow leaves that had collected in piles from the oak trees above them, and placed the handpicked bouquet of orchids he'd brought against the stone, sighing noiselessly. Orchids had been his mother's favorite kind of flower. He stayed kneeling in silence for a few seconds, the flowers rustling against each other from the strong autumn wind that coursed through the air.

"Your mother would be very proud of you, son." Sam Davenport said softly in his deep baritone voice. "You've landed your first job in the very same department where your mother and I launched our own careers, and where we first met. It feels like it was just yesterday when we were assigned our first case together..."

His son nodded. He didn't want to say what was really on his mind, so he let him continue.

"My one and only son: rookie investigator for the FBI. And soon maybe even director!" Sam boasted. He turned to face him. "We need to celebrate."

Jonah stood, shaking his head. "I'm not in the mood." he said, peering down at his mother's memorial. "I'm just gonna go home and get ready for my first day tomorrow."

Sam sensed his son's dismal mood but chose not to address it directly, although he did want him to feel as eager as he was. "Alright. But, at least let Lacey bake a cake, and maybe stop by the store and grab some champagne." he insisted, putting a firm hand on Jonah's shoulder. "You're in the big leagues now, son. Working in law enforcement in Ruxlor is no joke. Once you've experienced the career milestones your mother and I have endured for ourselves and what it took to earn them, maybe then you'll start celebrating."

Sam was a highly decorated senior detective for the Ruxlor City Police Department, but worked alongside the

FBI and sometimes collaborated on cases with them if needed. He started out as an investigator just like his son, then accepted a job offer at the police department a few years later, and quickly moved up the ranks to the high title that he held now. He had his own fair share of insane occurrences and near-death experiences. He knew that as an agent working tough and gritty cases, his son would no doubt come face to face with ruthless criminals—most of them seasoned killers and convicts—and would need to do whatever it took to hunt them down, just like his late wife Serena. She'd worked on the frontlines and in the shadows as an undercover cop, and Jonah grew up awestruck, hearing high-octane and action-packed stories from her work that sounded like grand adventures to his young mind's overactive imagination—high-speed car chases, county-wide manhunts, search and rescues, shootouts, drug busts, hostage situations. She suddenly and tragically lost her life during an undercover assignment busting a weapons-smuggling ring four years ago.

Jonah sighed. "Fine. Tell Lacey she can make a cake. But that's it."

Lacey was Sam's new wife. Jonah didn't have anything against her, she was nice and all and seemed to make Sam very happy, but the love and support she'd tried to give to him would never match the kind of love Serena had given him. He didn't have the warm feeling of unconditional love and emotional security as he'd felt with the woman that birthed him. Also, he just couldn't see how his father was able to jumpstart his grieving process and move on from Serena so quickly, even though a few years passed since they had lost her.

Jonah wished he knew how he did it; it still felt like it was just yesterday when he got the call...Didn't Sam still feel the same way? Wasn't his heart permanently bruised like his son's was? He didn't like the change, but lately that was what his life entailed. Change, change, and more change. He didn't appreciate it, but he knew that was how life worked and so he had to deal with it.

"Great." Sam smiled. "Just know that we're all proud of you, son. Not just Lacey and I, but the whole community. We just want to celebrate your success with you. You got a bright career ahead of you. Let's go."

They took their time walking back to Sam's black on black Cadillac Escalade, soaking up as much of the warm October sun as they could. When they climbed in and prepared to leave, Jonah's brand new work phone vibrated in his side pocket. He retrieved it, puzzled. The caller ID displayed his new boss's name: Bex Chapman. She was the director of the Criminal Profilers Unit within Ruxlor City's FBI Field Office. He answered the call.

"Davenport, am I interrupting anything?" Bex said urgently, omitting a formal greeting.

"No, ma'am." Jonah replied. "Not at all."

"Good. Then you've got your first job a day early. I'm sending the address now. We're thinking homicide. Be there ASAP."

She hung up without any further explanation. Jonah pocketed his phone.

"I'm guessing that was Chapman?" Sam said as he cruised away from the memorial grounds and turned onto the main road. He'd worked in a unit with her for a few months before he had gotten his offer to work for the police department.

"Yeah. I actually just got my first case." Jonah said, relieved to have an excuse not to go home with Sam and Lacey. It still felt like there was a missing puzzle piece in the home, and that was his mother's presence. It would probably always feel that way, it seemed. He was grateful for the distraction of his new job, and for the new lease he'd signed on the tiny but still functional bachelor pad in the heart of downtown.

"See? That's great news, son. The celebration can hold off until tomorrow. Now it's time to put in that work and get the job done."

• • •

Rayne Winters felt indifferent as the cab driver left the Pittsburgh International Airport and made the one-hour trip into the ever-bustling Ruxlor City. Although she had been hundreds of miles away at college for the last four years (and at FBI special agent training in Quantico, Virginia for five months after that), her feelings for the town hadn't changed at all.

She wasn't happy to be back, but she wasn't disappointed either; she was going to build a solid career here, and who knew? Maybe relocate to New York City or Los Angeles or Miami—she'd heard of some insane yet fascinating cases in those places—to move up the ranks and earn new titles and reach new career milestones...Or even go back to Quantico. She knew she wanted in on the excitement and action one day soon. But this was where it would have to start: the isolated but prosperous town where she'd grown up.

The cab driver slowed to a stop in front of a gray and white, modernly designed gated apartment community on the edge of the city. Rayne handed him a generous tip and stepped out of the SUV as he gathered her luggage for her. She thanked him and headed into the leasing office. After getting a shiny new key and a copy of the paperwork she had read over online just before her graduation day from FBI training, she made her way up to the tenth floor to what was going to be her new home.

The one-bedroom condominium she signed a lease on felt homey and inviting since the landlord let her keep all of the staging and furniture, and she switched on all of the lights and turned up the heat on the fancy touchscreen thermostat. The only thing that was missing was a TV, so she'd have to unpack in silence, which she wasn't too fond of. To her, silence was loud—deafening, even—and it only heightened her senses and made her paranoia worse. She couldn't understand how some people enjoyed complete silence at all.

As she unpacked, she was on a video call with her mother Neevah, a popular writer, and her father Owen, a journalist, who actually very conveniently lived down the street in a townhome in the same complex.

"We'll stop by tomorrow evening to help you." her father was saying. "I'm excited to see the place you picked out. Then we can start planning your graduation party."

"I appreciate it, Dad. It's actually pretty nice here." Rayne said. "How is work—?"

Suddenly, her cell phone buzzed in with an incoming call, and the caller ID replaced the video footage of her parents. It was Bex Chapman, director of the Criminal Profilers Unit, or CPU—her new boss. Rayne was her newest rookie agent, starting a career as a criminal profiler.

"Sorry, Dad, but I have to call you guys back. It's my boss."

"No worries, we'll talk to you later. We love you."

"Love you too."

She then answered Bex's call and lifted her cell phone up to her ear. "Hello?"

"Are you in the city yet?" Bex Chapman said hastily.

"Hi, uh, yeah. I actually just got in town about an hour ago. I'm just getting settled in." Rayne replied as she sat on a metal barstool and took a gulp of water from a condensating bottle.

"Don't. You've got your first case."

3

BEX CHAPMAN HAD TEXTED AN address to Rayne's phone, and she followed her car's GPS to the unknown destination. She drove an old silver BMW sedan that was formerly her father's, the motor humming and rattling in protest from not being driven in the years she was away at school. Her father kept it in the garage of their previous home and would start it up every week or so to keep it alive, but it still sounded like it was on the brink of collapse. When she arrived at the location, Rayne looked around to what appeared to be a small local radio station's headquarters, the parking lot dead empty except for one black convertible with a government license plate, which she assumed was Bex's. It was a small red building that was slightly rundown but still looked habitable for the most part, at least from the outside.

Rayne, now dressed in jeans, black boots, and a navy blue windbreaker jacket with the words FBI on the back in yellow text with her long, coily hair tucked under a matching FBI cap, stepped out of her car and made her way into the building.

She peered down a corridor to see Bex Chapman standing in front of an open doorway that was blocked off by yellow caution tape, and Rayne walked over to stand at her side. She smelled something burnt in the air.

"Be careful when you go in, Winters. Smoke's still permeating the air." Bex said. "They already took the body."

Rayne slipped on a pair of white latex gloves and held her breath for just a moment as she lifted the do-not-cross tape and stepped into the room that now reeked of burnt wood, singed paper, and thick smoke, and she immediately knew that something was off. Her vision of how this alleged homicide possibly could have taken place began to play in her head like a film as she envisioned several potential scenarios and outcomes. Bex stayed put in the hallway, watching her work in silence, knowing she'd picked the right person for this job; she'd been briefed on Rayne's stellar potential down at Quantico, and Rayne could pick up on things that even Bex's most seasoned agents couldn't, and she had an innate sense for reading suspects and the scenes of the crimes they'd fled from.

After a few more moments, Bex spoke first, crossing her arms over her chest. "Accident?"

Rayne shook her head. "No. Look." She pointed a gloved finger to seemingly randomized spots in the room that had been burned to ashes. "If this 'fire' was an accident, the flames would have spread around the room faster than the person would have been able to control. The flames would have eventually engulfed everything. Probably even the entire building, depending on what time the firemen would have arrived. The station itself is still completely intact and usable from what I've seen. Also, the only things in this room that were lost were a few file cabinets, some tech equipment, and the victim himself. These were controlled fires. The suspect had a bigger purpose than to just burn the entire place down."

"So, we can confirm to the police that this wasn't accidental?"

"I would say in this case, yes. They wouldn't have called us over here otherwise. It seems the suspect came in with all of the tools needed to accomplish his task, got to the victim first, then proceeded to destroy things that he or she didn't want us to see."

"We may have a skilled arsonist on our hands, then." Bex said.

"I think we might...Did we identity the victim?"

"The only person that was clocked in at the time of the crime was a middle-aged male named Evan Brentwood who hosts a local daytime radio show and produces here and there. Our forensics team is still working on him now just to make sure it's him, as well as looking for any form of DNA to identify a potential suspect. This scene is still fresh, so it's going to take about an hour or so for them to get the DNA reads back. I'll call your personal cell with any updates until my tech agents finish setting up your work phone. I think I made the right choice by bringing you onto my team. I appreciate you coming in on such short notice."

"It's not a problem. I appreciate it, Ms. Chapman."

"Please, just call me Bex or Chief. I'm not as formal as the other higher-ups around here." Bex was a tall, lean forty-something former Special Agent with short, spiky brunette hair, green eyes, and a physically fit figure from her glory days working undercover busting big-time criminals. "Obviously, I'll add this to your pay since it's technically after work hours and we're not at headquarters. But, I think our work here is done, so I'll get the forensics crew to take the rest of the evidence you pointed out back to the lab. The cleanup crew will handle the rest, and then..."

Bex was still talking, but Rayne was no longer listening. She was hearing footsteps.

Then abruptly, a voice: "Did the party start without me?"

She froze. *Wait*, she thought. *It can't be...is it?*

Rayne turned around to see someone she never thought she'd ever see again.

• • •

Jonah...

Time seemed to slow and eventually come to a stop as she took him in. *I really am looking at him...Is this real?*

It was indeed him. Jonah. He was here, in the same vicinity as her. He shared equal surprise, looking her up and down as if she were a ghost. Both of them were unable to process the appropriate words to say. What could they have said? It had been four years since they'd last exchanged words, embraced. Four years that'd felt like an achingly long eternity. Now that the eternity was over, neither of them knew what was to come next.

"You two know each other?" Bex didn't hide the perplexed expression on her face. She stood between the two agents now, looking back and forth at each of their faces. From the looks of it, they were neither elated nor annoyed to see each other.

Jonah Davenport was the first to respond, breaking his gaze. "Yeah, uh...we pretty much grew up together."

Rayne, still in shock, let out a long sigh and tried to keep a straight, emotionless face. "We do...we've known each other for a really long time, actually." The last time she'd seen him, she didn't tell him that she was packing her bags and leaving Ruxlor City behind for school then going straight to Quantico for FBI training afterward. At the time, she was certain she was leaving for good...They had made a pact to study criminology together at the community college, but Rayne had made a final, silent decision to move far away from the secluded metro town that they grew up in and experience a new life elsewhere. She hadn't said goodbye.

It wasn't because she didn't want to, but because it would have been too painful.

Looking at him now, he appeared slightly older but did not look too different, just more defined and mature-looking. He had no doubt changed on the outside, but she wondered if he changed on the inside too. Emotionally, rather. He lost his mother just before their high school graduation, which was another reason why she didn't break the news to him that she was leaving. She simply vanished and didn't come back.

Until today.

"Well, that's great!" Bex said, but the two rookies' faces did not match her enthusiasm. "I always tell my agents: the stronger the bond they have with each other, the better they'll work as a team, and the more trust they'll have in each other. We're like each other's second family, especially when things get rough with a case. You'll see that tomorrow morning when you meet everyone at headquarters."

Rayne averted her gaze from Jonah's dejected eyes and cleared her throat. "I have to go, but thank you for assigning me to this case, Bex. I appreciate you putting your trust in me to help solve this." She began to walk out of the room, and she looked up at Jonah one more time. "Goodbye, Jonah." she said softly.

"See you tomorrow, rookie." Jonah replied with a small, forced smile as he watched her go. When Rayne was gone, he turned to Bex. "Did I miss anything crucial?"

Bex shook her head. "Not at all. I just wanted you to shadow my own analysis of the murder, but Winters beat you to it. We wrapped things up pretty quickly. We'll all come together and go over the findings in the morning as a unit."

Jonah nodded, scanning the recording studio over once more before inputting his own thoughts to Bex, who eagerly jotted them down in a small notepad, and he left the scene.

• • •

The church bells rang five times, indicating that it had just struck five o'clock in the evening. The sun was beginning to dip below the horizon, casting a pink and orange hue in the sky above them. It was an unbearably hot evening, although it was only mid-April, but they sat outside in the radiating heat anyway, separating themselves from everyone else inside the church. Neither of them said anything for a while as they watched cars zip past and passersby walking in all directions to their destinations. The usual sounds of the ever-bustling city surrounded them.

Rayne spoke first. "Are you sure this is still a life you want?" she whispered.

Jonah's brown eyes glistened with intensity as he stared into her own tear-filled gaze. "Absolutely. This is what I want to do. I want to hunt down criminals and make them pay for what they do—including the guys who did this to my mom. I'm going to keep her name alive and keep my dream of being an agent just like her. She was tough, resilient, hardworking, caring, and everybody respected her. She was my idol for as long as I can remember. I won't let her death go unavenged."

She pulled him into a tight embrace where they sat, wrapping her arms around his neck, and his own arms slinked around her waist. They stayed there for a long time, crying noiselessly together, until he pulled back slightly, their foreheads almost touching. "I, uh, I should've told you this before, but—"

Everything faded as Rayne woke up, the memory dissolving into nothing.

Huffing, she reached over the annoyingly large California king-sized bed and grabbed her phone off the diamond-encrusted nightstand. She checked the time. 5:02 A.M. It was three hours before she had to report for her first day on the job, but she knew that once she was up, she wouldn't be able to fall back asleep anytime soon. She wasn't nervous about starting her career with the Ruxlor City FBI Field Office. At least, not until she saw Jonah Davenport again for the first time in years. She hadn't given him a proper goodbye, didn't even given him the chance to tell her everything he'd needed to say at that point in time, and now they were going to be working side by side on the city's toughest and most dangerous cases.

Their sudden and unanticipated reunion was going to hinder both of them emotionally, she knew that, and Rayne didn't want that at all; this was a big opportunity and a stepping stone for both of their reputations and careers, so ultimately they were going to have to come to an agreement; they were going to need to put the past aside and put one hundred percent of their focus into this crime. They were dealing with a potential murder case as their very first assignment, and they needed to find out who did it, and why...

Putting the past behind them, however, was much easier said than done.

35

4

RAYNE SHOWERED, DRESSED IN ATHLETIC attire, and completed her rigorous thirty-minute workout routine she'd perfected at her time away at college before making a quick and simple breakfast that consisted of maple oatmeal, an assortment of fruits, and vanilla-flavored coffee. But as the time crept closer to eight o'clock, the sun beginning to emerge above a serene pink and blue horizon, a feeling of dread sank in the pit of her stomach. She felt terrible. Ill, actually, even though she did nothing at all; all she did was leave. But not doing anything was probably the worst thing she could have done. This day was supposed to be exciting, but now she wanted it to be over already.

Upon finishing her breakfast, Rayne stepped into the master bathroom and couldn't help but sigh when she saw her face in the mirror. *I look terrible*, she thought as she began applying makeup. It wasn't anything overly noticeable, just some light enhancements to make her appear more put together and not like she was living off of a few hours of sleep; mascara, concealer, nude-toned lip gloss. Pleased with the final look, she thought it definitely helped hide the fact that she didn't sleep very well the night before, but her eyes told a different story. It was said that one's eyes were a gateway to their soul, and looking at her own eyes, Rayne saw a dispirited yet highly anxious person.

She tried to shake it off and force herself to get into a positive headspace as she dressed in an outfit similar to what she wore yesterday at the radio station. It was twenty degrees colder this morning than it was yesterday, and Rayne didn't know if she was going to have to leave the field office and revisit the crime scene, so she dressed warmly: beige dress pants, form-fitting black turtleneck, stylish black boots, completed with her FBI windbreaker and matching baseball cap. Today she pulled her curls into a low ponytail that cascaded down just past her shoulder blades. She grabbed her keys and headed out the door, determined to turn the day around.

• • •

Jonah accessorized his simple black pants and fitted black T-shirt that showed off his toned figure with his mother's shiny cross emblem that hung from a thick gold chain, and a gold Michael Kors watch that was a high school graduation present from his father. Since there was a bitter chill in the air this morning, he put on his FBI jacket and zipped it up to his chin. He smoothed over the sleeves and adjusted his watch.

"You sure it was her?" Sam asked. He was also preparing to leave, dressed in a gray suit with a dark blue tie that he was fastening in the mirror in front of them. "Rayne Winters?"

Jonah nodded. "Yeah, it was her alright. She's a profiler, I'm a detective. Just like we planned to be..." Jonah had stopped by his childhood home to have breakfast with Sam and Lacey before his big first day, and had filled Sam in on what went down the evening before. Sam was aware of how deep his son's feelings still were for her, even all these years later; Jonah had originally confessed it to him after Rayne originally went to their senior prom with a guy that wasn't him. Seeing her shine in a sparkling ivory colored designer dress and professionally done makeup but noticing how she wasn't really having much fun at the dance, Jonah admitted to his dad that he told her how he really felt and convinced Rayne to ditch her friends and the dance, sneaking out and taking the Porsche rental that Serena had surprised him with and speeding away from the hotel as if they were getaway drivers, adventuring around the city and getting into mischief. They ended up at the popular Blue Valley Park Grounds at a breathtaking picnic area that overlooked the twinkling city. It was that night when they both realized that their friendship wouldn't quite be the same by morning.

He'd asked Sam for advice the next day, and he told Jonah confidently, "Just go for it, son. That's what I did with your mother. Serena's strong, tough, and sometimes stubborn. It took some convincing, but she finally let me take her on a date, and the rest is history."

He also asked his mother the same thing. If only he knew it would have been the last piece of advice she'd give him. "Show her how much you care about her. But not only that, show her the lengths in which you'll go to make sure she's happy, well cared for, and safe Just be yourself, and everything else will fall into place. You two already know each other very well and have a strong bond from your friendship. Your love for each other will only blossom from there."

"Well, what are you going to do? You still value your friendship, right? Do you think it's worth salvaging?" Sam asked, glancing at his son in the mirror.

"Of course I still value it. It's just...strange seeing her come back, I guess. It's complicated, that's all." Jonah said with finality. "I'm not going to confront her about it, but I know it's going to have to happen sooner or later. Now that she's apparently living here in Ruxlor again, that's all I think about."

"I believe in you, son. Just don't let it cloud your head too much; remember, you're in the big leagues now—both of you are. You and Rayne can still prosper and make names for yourselves regardless of what happens."

Jonah nodded, but that piece of advice didn't soothe him in that moment. Seeing Rayne at the radio station sent his mind into overdrive. He couldn't help but overthink, he had so many questions and so few answers. He sighed heavily as he spritzed a little extra cologne on himself before grabbing his car keys and heading out the door behind Sam, remembering Serena's endearing words.

• • •

A beaming Bex Chapman was waiting for her newest agents as they walked up to the front entrance of the Ruxlor City FBI Field Office.

"'Morning, rookies." Bex said and clasped her hands together. "Your new squad is eager to meet both of you, and they can't wait to get their hands on this case. Figuratively, not literally. It's been pretty slow these past few weeks so things are about to get pretty interesting. Anyways, follow me.”

Jonah and Rayne awkwardly glanced at each other then looked away as they followed Bex up the concrete steps and into the lobby of the gray building. The field office was approximately ten thousand square feet, and the lobby alone was open and expansive. They walked back to the north wing of the first floor and down a brightly lit hallway. They stopped at a newly installed frosted glass door that was labeled ‘CPU.’ Criminal Profilers Unit.

“I got the green light to start my own subdivision of our city’s Violent Crimes Unit not too long ago, actually. I decided to name it the Criminal Profiling Unit.” Bex explained as she tapped her ID badge that was clipped to her chest on the scanner that was beside the doorknob, and the light turned green, the door unlocked. “I think having our very own criminal profiling team will help not just our friends over at Violent Crimes but the entire FBI field office in every aspect of our jobs. I proposed my idea to the director, and surprisingly he approved my idea. In this city, we need people that can get into these criminals’ heads, predict their next moves, get ten steps ahead of them. And I think you guys can do just that. Welcome to the CPU.” She ushered them inside. “This suite is where my unit works around the clock, and where you two will be spending a lot of your time.

We've got two brand new computer labs, a forensics lab, kitchen and dining area for breaks, a lounge with a nice big TV, a conference room for when we do collab investigations, private research rooms if you need some time alone, et cetera. I'm going to grab my team so we can do a formal introduction."

At that, Bex disappeared into a connecting room. A few moments later she returned, followed by six other agents all dressed in their expected uniform: shined black shoes, black dress pants, some with belts, and tucked in navy blue t-shirts. Some wore the same baseball caps or jackets that the rookies had received. Bex began by introducing the rookies first, then her agents.

"CPU, I am very honored to bring in my two newest recruits to start within our team, effective immediately. I have Jonah Davenport, graduated from Ruxlor College, completed the police academy also. He will be our newest investigator. Some of you may already know his father, Sam, the senior detective for the Ruxlor City PD. I also brought in my second recruit, Rayne Winters: graduated from George Washington University, the police academy, then trained at Quantico. She'll be my newest profiler."

"This is exciting." one of the female agents said cheerfully. "The more agents the merrier."

"These," Bex motioned to the two agents standing closest to her, "are who I like to call my tech geeks: Agents Anisa Ray and Keon Toussaint. If we need to trace phone calls, get into suspects' or victims' email addresses, personal devices, hard drives, decrypt a code—basically find out absolutely anything we need to know about their identities or things they were trying to hide, these are our guys."

Both Anisa and Keon held gray tablets in their hands, and gave courteous nods to the newest additions.

"Special Agent Leigh Crenshaw," Bex pointed to a redheaded woman in the middle of the group, "is our only criminal psychologist as of right now, but she's a jack of all trades; psychoanalyst, interrogator, can go undercover if I need her to. She's proven that she can do whatever it takes to close a case."

Bex introduced three more agents, detective Diana Reeves, profiler Roscoe Hall, and forensics analyst Sawyer Blackridge, before showing the rookies where their new cubicles had been set up, ironically right next to each other, which was where they would be doing most of their work when they weren't outside of headquarters. After giving them a rundown of the features and equipment the techs gave them access to, Bex told them they were going to be conducting their daily morning agenda meeting in the first conference room.

Bex spoke while the three of them walked down to the conference room. "Every morning at 8:30 sharp is our daily agenda meeting. This is when we talk about our individual and group progress with any cases that we've been assigned, breakthroughs or things that we're stumped on, tasks that need to get done by the end of the day, and whatnot. This helps us all stay on the same page and keep each other up to speed. We also meet one more time at 3:30 then try to be out the door for the night at four o'clock."

The rest of the team was already seated in the room when they arrived, their laptops and notepads set up in front of them. The conference space had one large whiteboard next to a 70-inch flatscreen television at the front of the room, a circular glass table in the middle of the area with about ten swivel chairs, a filtered water machine in the corner, and a few file cabinets. Bex sat in the chair closest to the television and grabbed a remote to turn it on. "We're going to skip the good-mornings and get right into it." she stated as Agent Sawyer Blackridge spread out blown-up, laminated images of the crime scene on the table so everyone could see them. "Leigh is going to give her take on these images, then we'll determine what direction we want to go in regarding this case."

Special Agent Leigh Crenshaw stood and synced her tablet screen to the TV on the wall, displaying one digital image at a time, each with her handwritten notes on the side. "Well, for starters, I can definitely see why the PD wanted this to go straight to us; clearly, our suspect wanted something—or someone—to disappear. "Why didn't the whole room burn down? What could possibly explain why he or she only created small, controlled fires using an array of chemicals in very specific areas and on certain objects in the room, and not destroy the whole building like previous arsonists we've handled? Also, Sawyer got the DNA reads back last night, and it definitely was Evan Brentwood's body. We don't know if he was just in the wrong place at the wrong time or was intentionally targeted, but either way he'd dead, and now the perpetrator will be tried for murder."

Jonah nodded, taking it all in. "We need to figure out what exactly they got rid of. That'll help us uncover the motive and catch the right person, and see if the victim was supposed to be killed or not."

"That's right," Rayne said. "We should go through Mr. Brentwood's phone records to see what he was doing around the time of the incident." She couldn't help it, but she didn't want Jonah to outshine her—if that was what he was even doing.

"I'm on it." Keon Toussaint said. "Anisa and I will have his records ready within the next few hours."

When the morning agenda concluded, Rayne and Jonah had no problems fitting into the team's typical routine as they shadowed their work, collaborating often, comparing notes and formulating a plan of action to present to Bex at the end of the work day. To each of their own unspoken satisfaction, they'd kept each other at a safe distance physically as they were able to finalize a small list of people to start interviewing regarding Evan Brentwood's death. Although, it did grow harder to keep themselves contained as the hours dragged on. Every now and then they would catch themselves, glancing and locking gazes, brushing fingertips. Each time was only for a half of a second, if that, but to them it felt like time was standing still again.

• • •

Rayne caught up with Jonah just as he clocked out in the break room and was about to turn and leave the field office.

She took his hand before he could begin to walk. "Wait, I need to talk to you, before you go…"

"…You don't." he said softly, stopping just a few inches in front of her. His doe-brown eyes glistened. "At least, not today. Not here, and not right now. When the time is right, you'll know where to find me." At that, he squeezed her hand twice, like a single heartbeat—a gesture she hadn't felt in so long—and he let his hand drop back down to his side as he left the room, not looking back at her.

"I'm sorry." she called after him.

He paused, nodded, and continued to walk out into the night.

5

SPECIAL AGENT LEIGH CRENSHAW MET UP with Jonah and Rayne at the FBI field office early the next morning. She set a box of a dozen assorted donuts on the glass table before them, and handed each of them a styrofoam cup of steaming hot black coffee. They thanked her and opened up their files.

"So, what do you think about this list?" Rayne asked, referring to the short list of suspects Bex had her and Jonah had compile after reviewing the victim's recent cell phone records, text messages, emails, and known physical encounters.

"Well," Leigh skimmed over the paper in front of her, "from face value it looks like this guy didn't really have a lot of close friends or relatives. He had a solid reputation at that radio station, but he wasn't really close with anyone there either. Hopefully the people I bring in will spill some info about his life and any recent whereabouts that we should be aware of."

"What about security footage?" Jonah asked. "Did the owner of the building have any cameras set up inside or outside the premises?"

Leigh shook her head. "Unfortunately not. It looked like they were all cut off right before the incident happened. It's as if someone strategically plotted this out and didn't want anyone to see it. Whoever we're dealing with, they know what they're doing. But it won't necessarily make them harder to catch, though."

That fact didn't deter Rayne, nor did it daunt Jonah. Like Leigh and the rest of the team, they were all determined to find the one responsible for this.

Rayne stood. "Well, let's get to work."

Leigh led the rookies to the two interrogation rooms their building had. The first name on the list was Lana, Evan Brentwood's ex-wife, but Leigh could instantly tell by the woman's body language that she was not the one they were looking for. But she reminded herself not to let this woman slip past her either. Nothing was always as it seemed. "I'm going to ask her a few questions, and you guys watch how I do it." Leigh instructed. "It's always good to speak with relatives and other loved ones; I need to read her and note how she reacts to what I say."

"Better to be safe than sorry." Jonah stated.

"Correct. Sit here so you guys can listen in on it and take notes if you wish. This won't take me very long." Leigh grabbed a manila file folder that was stuffed with the forensic unit's photographs of the scene of the crime and stepped into the first interrogation room, where Lana was sitting at a steel table, dabbing underneath her eyes with a crinkled tissue.

"Good morning, ma'am. I'm Special Agent Leigh Crenshaw from the Violent Crimes Unit. You must be Miss Lana...?"

"My maiden name is Abbott, but I never bothered going through the hassle to get it changed back." Lana chuckled coldly.

"Ms. Abbott." They shook hands and Leigh sat down across from her, setting the manila folder on the table in between them. "I'm sorry we have to meet under these circumstances. I'm currently overseeing the Criminal Profiling division, and it's going to be my team's job to find the person responsible for this."

"Evan and I had our differences, and we downright hated each other by the end of our marriage, but...he didn't deserve to be murdered. Especially not like that." Lana said.

The rookies could hear the muffled voices on the other side of the one-way glass window. Lana Brentwood was teary-eyed and had gone pale after seeing the gorey photographs, but she wasn't hysterical. However, it was to be expected; Leigh had learned during her pleasantly casual interview with Lana Abbott that she and Evan had only been married for three years and divorced for six. Time had caused the few good memories of their short-lived union to fade, and both parties had moved on long before the ink on the divorce papers dried.

"When you were with him," Leigh said. "do you recall anyone having a bone to pick with Evan? Did he have any bad relations or have altercations with anyone that you can think of?"

"A lot of people didn't like Evan, but he was respected at his job and at the country club we had a membership at. He had his small circle of friends, as did I, but he still liked to keep his business to himself." Lana explained.

"And why was that? Being unliked, I mean."

"He was greedy, money-hungry. Only cared about benefiting himself. He could've had many flourishing relationships throughout his career, but he ruined it for himself."

"Do you know if anything had happened recently regarding a new endeavor in his personal life or work life?"

"Not at all. Look, I'm going to be honest with you, I'm probably not going to be much help with all this investigation stuff. Even when we were together he never kept me updated on those kinds of things. I was just a trophy wife, nothing more. It annoyed me after the first year. It wasn't until our divorce I was able to pick up my own career again."

"Well, any help is good help. My team still appreciates you coming in this morning, Ms. Abbott. You've provided good information. We're all finished here, but if you remember anything at all that you think we should be aware of, please don't hesitate to call. Here's my card." Leigh handed her a business card with the Criminal Profilers Unit's contact information on it, and an officer escorted Lana out of the interrogation room.

When Leigh exited the room, Bex appeared and walked up to the trio swiftly.

"Another fire was just reported in a business plaza on McAllister Road. One victim. Nothing triggered the fire. The Ruxlor City Police Department is handing this one over to us too. Davenport, I'm sending you with Agent Hall and the forensics crew to shadow them. Take notes and stay alert."

"I'm on it." Jonah was visibly eager to get out of the office and spring into action, and he wasted no time leaving Leigh and Rayne behind.

• • •

"Miss Alistair! Will you sign my book?"

Neevah sat with her husband at The Lighthouse, a posh and rather expensive seafood restaurant in the heart of the city, waiting for their daughter to join them for dinner. The dress code was semi-formal, so Neevah dressed in a ruby-red pantsuit and razor-sharp stiletto heels, her hair pinned into an updo, Owen remaining in the black suit he wore to work. Their waitress, awestruck to be waiting on her table, rushed up to them clutching Neevah's latest true-crime publication, *Sleeping With the Enemy*, beaming.

"Of course, dear. Have a pen?" Neevah didn't mind doing impromptu book signings, she was always open to meeting new readers wherever she went and it kept her encouraged as a writer, and she signed her swift signature that she could probably do with her eyes closed. She handed the hardcover back to the waitress.

"Thank you so much!" the young woman smiled.

"Anytime, thank you for reading." Neevah replied. The waitress turned and scurried back into the kitchen, bringing out their drinks a few moments later, and Neevah and Owen perused the menu. When their daughter arrived at the table, they were elated.

"My dear, you look beautiful." Neevah stood to hug her only child, Owen following. She was happy to see Rayne safe and sound after the bouts of paranoia she'd been battling since returning to the city.

"I'm so happy we're all back home." Rayne said. She was dressed in a black ankle-length designer dress with shiny heels, complete with shimmering diamond earrings and an elegant matching necklace, scarlet-red lipstick and silver eyeshadow. It was nice to be out of her FBI gear for a while, but she was eager to be back on the clock tomorrow. She couldn't wait to tell her parents about her first official day as a profiler in training. Rayne sat down and shared a menu with her father, which instantly made her mouth water; she hadn't eaten at this place since before she moved away, and the memories of the fresh and savory dishes came back to her quickly.

While they waited for their appetizers, Rayne couldn't help but wonder what exactly Jonah was doing while he was shadowing Agent Hall and the forensics crew. She wished she was also getting extra hands-on experience, but then she caught herself stewing in jealousy. It's only the first day, she told herself. I'll put my skills to use soon enough. She knew Bex made her decisions with good reasoning. When she needed her, she'd surely call. Hopefully Jonah and the others would discover more clues and, if they were lucky, fingerprints, a hair, anything that could lead them to identifying their perpetrator.

"So, Mom, did your publisher give you a contract for your next book yet?" Rayne wanted to hear about her parents' lives before talking about her own.

"Almost. We're negotiating it as we speak." Neevah said.

"Dad, anything cool happen while reporting today?" Rayne asked.

"Not that I can think of, but we want to know about you." Owen smiled. "Our daughter, an FBI agent! How was the first day on the job?"

"Oh, and how is Jonah doing over there?" Neevah said. "I saw his father's post on Facebook that he also got the position. I hope he's adjusting well to the unit. It must be hard knowing Serena worked in the same building."

"He's...good." Rayne murmured, taking a long sip from her glass of water.

"That is so wonderful that the two of you get to work together. I still have those pictures of you guys playing in your matching police officer Halloween costumes when you were in kindergarten. Time goes by so fast."

Rayne sighed. "Yeah, I remember." She needed to change the subject. "Speaking of, we already got assigned to not one, but two cases. Bex must have a lot of faith in us already."

"Interesting." Neevah's eyebrows raised. "Are you allowed to discuss it?"

"Somewhat. We've got a pretty interesting suspect. I've never studied anything quite like this in school."

"How so?" Owen asked.

"He—assuming he's a male—burned two victims and left their bodies wherever they fell, not trying to hide his crimes at all, and created small, controllable fires within a twenty-foot radius, destroying anything he didn't want us to find."

Both Neevah and Owen froze. Neevah almost lost her grip on her fork, and she slowly placed it beside her plate. She cleared her throat.

"Mom, are you alright? You look like you just saw a ghost." their daughter laughed and continued eating.

Neevah forced her heart rate to steady and tried to smile as naturally as she could, hoping Rayne didn't see the pure shock in her eyes. "Yes, of course. That just sounds...peculiar, is all. What else do you know about it?"

"That's pretty much it. We didn't want to jump to any conclusions—until we got the call for the second murder a few hours ago. Jonah's shadowing the crime scene right now. We think they're linked, but as of right now there's no similarities between the victims whatsoever. But I'm sure we'll find a connection soon, it's only the first day."

Neevah and Owen exchanged a worried glance that Rayne didn't catch.

6

NEEVAH AND OWEN WEREN'T GOING HOME. They traveled down Maxwell Run Highway, en route to Neevah's sister's mansion that lied just outside the county line. They were both on edge after hearing their daughter's shocking words.

"This isn't happening." Neevah kept telling herself. "This is not happening. What if..." She couldn't finish her sentence, unable to fathom it. A knot formed in the pit of her stomach.

"We don't know anything for sure." Owen replied, but his voice didn't sound nearly as reassuring as Neevah would have liked. "We should tell her about the deal—"

"We will not be telling her about anything. If she doesn't remember, then we're going to keep it that way."

"We could give Chapman a call and tell her to assign Rayne to a different case."

"No, no. That'll only make Rayne suspect that something's going on. Besides, she looked really excited to be contributing to the team. We can let her work without us interfering, but stay alert."

"But if something happens or she gets too close—"

"Then we'll do everything in our power to stop that from happening."

Owen did not add anything else. They arrived at the security gate at the pristinely manicured entrance to Cliffmont Estates ten minutes later and waited for Neevah's sister to buzz them in. He gulped. "While we're here, we should at least convince her to change her mind about the deal."

"You know she's not going to do that." Neevah almost chuckled. "When she's fixated on something, especially something that will boost her ego or her reputation, she'll hold onto it and won't let it go. She'll make sure she sees this through. My sister always gets what she wants."

• • •

Simone Alistair was enjoying this a bit too much, Neevah knew that for sure. They were supposed to be doing this for the sake of justice, and justice only. The stakes were already high enough, why didn't she see that?

"You shouldn't want fame out of this, Simone." Neevah said in a low tone. Neevah, Owen, Simone, along with her fiancé Miguel, sat at a thousand-dollar glass dining table, sipping white wine. Well, Simone and Miguel were drinking. Neevah and Owen hadn't touched their glasses.

"Fame isn't something I go out of my way to get, dear sister." Simone said smoothly. "It just comes to me. I couldn't help but become a phenomenon after the interview we did when we were teenagers, and when I accepted that seven-figure book deal last month. Someone has to tell our family's story. And if it isn't going to be you, then it's only fair that I step up and take the opportunity. Now look where it's gotten me." She motioned around her lavish home, glass still in hand. "I honestly didn't ask for all of this, but I'm certainly not going to reject it."

"You have to call everything off." Neevah said sternly. "Something bad is going to come from this, I know it."

"What about you, Neevah? Why do I have to change my mind?"

"We've already rethought our decision to do this." Owen said. "Now it's time for you to rethink yours."

"I don't see what all the fuss is about." Simone said. "What is going on?"

"Rayne is involved now!" Neevah said. "She is involved with a new string of murders that are very similar to the ones we know about. We cannot afford to put her in danger—"

"And what does any of this have to do with her job?" Simone shrugged. She harnessed the urge to roll her eyes as she took another sip of her wine. "This is what she's getting paid to do. Solve crimes. Close cases. Maybe she'll be the one to finally find him—"

"I don't want her in that madman's sights at all! We should have never agreed to open this back up. This is happening because of us."

Simone stood. "Rayne is fine and she can handle herself. I'm not backing out of this, Neevah. If you're so worried about her, go down to the field office and explain everything to her yourself. Tell her what happened when we were teenagers. And while you're at it, tell her how you failed to bring an end to this! She's an adult now—she's an FBI agent, for crying out loud."

"I'm not telling her anything," Neevah said with finality. "and you won't either." Not getting anywhere, she grabbed her purse and stormed out of the room. Owen got up and followed after her.

• • •

"Patrice Latimore." Leigh Crenshaw said as she pointed at the television screen the next morning, leading the team's daily briefing. The victim's state ID card was enlarged on the screen. "Thirty-nine years old, lived in Pittsburgh her whole life, well-respected in community volunteering and worked as a senior investigative journalist for Minto Media's newsroom. Her body was left torched in the middle of her living room, her work belongings missing. Who would want her dead, and why? And where is her work computer?"

"There were sensitive files on her laptop, I assume?" Detective Diana Reeves said.

"Yes, that was her work computer, and the techs over at Minto Media think the tracking chip was purposefully broken." Leigh responded.

"I was comparing Latimore's file to Evan Brentwood's, and there are no similarities whatsoever between the two of them." profiler Roscoe Hall said.

"But, they were both killed in the same style." Diana added. "There's more to a person than what's on the surface, so one of them is more than likely hiding something. Something's telling me these weren't just random serial murders."

Rayne sat in the middle of the table, soaking everything in. She was stunned at the fact that they were already at two victims in less than forty-eight hours; she'd only read about these cases in books and true crime blogs, and now she was living it. This was real life now.

Bex shook her head. "We need stronger leads. There had to have been a witness during at least one out of the two incidents."

"The police's reports claim there was no bystanders outside at all." Leigh reminded. "When they arrived at both scenes, they were ghost towns."

"I think we need to keep digging into the victims' records first and see what else we can find." Diana said. The other agents nodded, non-verbally agreeing.

Rayne raised her hand. "I can go interview people in the neighborhoods where the crimes happened while they're working on the intel."

Bex obliged. "Alright, Winters, you're on it. Everyone else, I want in-depth progress reports on my desk by five p.m. this evening to take to the chief of police." Her team nodded and swiftly began packing up their things.

"Bad idea. She's not going alone." Jonah interjected, already closing his laptop and standing up.

"And why not?" Rayne said, crossing her arms.

"No worries. Davenport can patrol the areas on standby." Bex said. "It's unlikely that something will go down at this time of the morning considering both murders happened at night, but having backup is never a bad thing. I want your findings presented to me by noon."

"Yes, ma'am." Rayne confirmed as she grabbed her bag and headed out of the conference room before Jonah could follow her.

•••

The upper-class neighborhood of McAllister in Ruxlor County was quaint and serene as Rayne drove her BMW down the wide roads that were lined with maple trees. The large homes had adequate space in between them and vast woodlands that seemed to span for miles behind them. Before venturing to Patrice Latimore's neighborhood, she decided to pay a visit to her boss first to try and get an idea on what could have possibly been on her work computer that someone had killed to have.

She parked on the street in front of the Acadian-style house and got out of her car, notepad and pen in hand. She also had a .25 in her holster, but she knew she wouldn't be using it.

Taking a quick glance behind her, she saw a black Dodge Charger come to a slow stop and park at the intersection about a block away. She knew it was Jonah, fulfilling their commander's orders as waiting on standby, just in case she would need backup for any reason. Rayne sighed and started up the concrete steps to the front door. She rang the electronic doorbell and waited.

"What do you want?" a man's gravelly voice said through the tiny speaker in the doorbell. He sounded instantly irritated.

"I'm Agent Rayne Winters from Violent Crimes over at the FBI field office." Rayne said. "I just need to ask you a few questions, if you don't mind." *Don't be too nice*, she reminded herself. *Nice never gets the job done.*

About a minute later the door opened, revealing a polished man in a gray plaid suit and dress shoes, headphones on. She'd assumed he was probably on a work conference call, as he was the director of a popular news company.

Rayne flashed her badge as she'd learned. "Detective Winters. Are you Dave Eckert, CEO of Minto Media?"

"Yeah." Dave jutted out his chin, narrowing his eyes at her. "Is this about Patrice?"

"Yes. I just need to ask you a few questions about her last assignment."

Dave removed his headphones and let them rest around his neck. He sighed as he powered them off by holding in a button of the side of the device. "I didn't assign Patrice that story. I usually am the one that gives her stories to cover, but this time I approved her own idea and let her take the lead."

"What was the story?" Rayne questioned.

Dave looked past her and to the area around them, although no one else was outside. For a moment, he was silent. "She did an evening story on that serial killer from ages ago. The guy from Humble Creek. At first I thought it was a stupid idea, but Patrice was really passionate about seeing the victims' families and doing a column on them for the anniversary. We cover local happenings, and Humble Creek is right in our county, so I gave the greenlight."

Rayne jotted everything down. "And details of her story were on her computer?"

"Most likely. All of the data on my employees' laptops syncs to one shared hard drive at headquarters, so I see everything that goes on, but for some reason we can't get into her account anymore. All of her contributions that she ever made to the company are completely wiped out."

"Did you look at any of her research before she was killed?"

"No. Patrice was one of my top journalists, so I didn't need to hover over her. I knew that she knew what she was doing. I was pondering skimming over some of her work, but the next day I got the call that she was dead."

"So you wouldn't know any of the names of the people she interviewed for her story?"

"I'm afraid not. I do apologize, Detective, but I have to go. I have a company to run."

At that, Dave turned away and closed the door.

• • •

Valencia, just thirty minutes north of Pittsburgh, was a tiny and quiet borough. Rayne turned onto Dodds Avenue and parked halfway down the short road. Getting out of her car and looking around, she could now see how there may not have been witnesses to see or hear Patrice Latimore's demise; thick woods separated each ranch and bungalow-style home, including Patrice's small house, and there were no streetlights anywhere. The incident occurred in the middle of the night, so Rayne had assumed the neighborhood would have been pitch-black omit an eerie orange glow coming from the house. But if no one was outside at the time of the event, which there likely wasn't, then no one would have noticed.

Rayne heard the car's tires against the rocky, unpaved road as it parked behind her. A door swung open and then slammed shut, and she could feel his presence as he stood behind her.

"I doubt we'll have much luck out here." Jonah said as he scanned the area.

To her dismay, he was right. They visited all of the houses on little Dodds Avenue and surrounding residential streets, and no one answered their doors. They got the occasional squint through living room blinds and threats through screen doors to stay out of their town. The residents of Valencia wanted nothing to do with them. They didn't blame them; a beloved staple of their community had been found dead in her own home from gruesome circumstances. Who could have committed such a heinous act? For what purpose? They didn't want to be involved in anything that was unfolding.

"Did Latimore's boss spill anything while you were questioning him?" Jonah asked as they were walking away from the final house they'd attempted. It lied alone down a private dirt road, somewhat set apart from the rest of the neighborhood. "Anything useful?"

"Just that Patrice was working on a story about past serial murders." Rayne said. "I wrote it all down for Bex. But, Dave Eckert didn't know any details because he said he trusted Patrice's process and she was one of his best workers, and the story didn't make it to the papers yet."

"If Eckert didn't look at her story before it was stolen, and no one else knew she was writing it, then who could've known to take her work computer from her house?"

"I don't know—"

Just then, there was a loud rustling coming from behind them, not too far into the woods. It was as if something—or someone—was stepping on twigs and crushing leaves. They turned around and froze, straining their ears to listen.

"Who's there?" Jonah boomed. He pulled out his gun and aimed it into the woods in one swift motion, taking a few steps towards the commotion. But there was no more noise, and no one in sight. All was quiet again.

"Can you relax a little? It's probably a deer." Rayne said.

Jonah huffed and pocketed his gun. "Let's get out of here." he muttered.

PART TWO

7

"NOT ONE PERSON TALKED?"

Bex Chapman sat behind her desk in her pristine and modernly designed office, peering up at her two agents through her wire-rimmed reading glasses.

"No, ma'am," Jonah replied somberly. Rayne shook her head.

Bex closed the manila file folder in front of her and drummed her fingers on the desk. She sighed. "And what did Mr. Eckert have to say?"

"He only told me that Patrice reached out to him about doing a news story about the anniversary of serial murders that happened around here," Rayne explained, "and that he approved it, but never got to see its progress before the computer disappeared."

Bex pondered for a moment. "I have a feeling we're going to end up getting a search warrant for Minto Media's building; Latimore had to have had some kind of physical notes or files on her story. I'm not letting him walk away from this just yet. I appreciate the report, Agents." She dismissed them with a short wave of her hand as she picked up the phone to call the city police department.

By the time the end of the day came, Rayne wasn't ready to pack up her thoughts and put everything away just yet as she sat in her cubicle, browsing over files that were sent to her from Anisa and Keon. They mostly contained pieces of information regarding their two victims, schooling, social reputations, accolades, work history, family history. She'd wanted to reach a breakthrough before clocking out, but as the time crept to 4:30 p.m. she knew it was very unlikely to happen today. All she needed was one connection, then the puzzle pieces would start to come together. Or, at least she hoped.

She locked her account on the desktop monitor before tossing her belongings into her satchel and grabbing her car keys. She stood from her desk and was about to leave the room when she spotted one person still staying behind while the rest of the day staff began to file out of the office.

"Still digging too?" Rayne leaned against the six-foot tall dividing wall of the cubicle, and Jonah's curly head popped up from his notes.

"Yeah, but racking my brain isn't going to do me any good." he mumbled as he closed his laptop. "I guess we'll have to look at everything from a fresh angle in the morning during the briefing." He stood.

"We can discuss some things over dinner and present what we know to the rest of the team in the morning?" Rayne suggested, trying to make her words sound nonchalant.

Jonah looked at her for a few seconds. As much as it pained him to see her, he knew he couldn't stay away from her forever. Neither of them could. As long as they both worked for Ruxlor City's Federal Bureau of Investigation, they were stuck together. "I guess we could." It beat eating cold leftover pizza in his equally cold and empty apartment, or going over to his father's house for dinner. "How about our usual spot at six?"

Rayne blinked. "Our usual...Oh right, Golden Lantern." She was surprised he'd even suggested their former favorite restaurant that they frequented as teens. *Maybe that's a good sign?* she thought to herself. "Yeah. That sounds perfect."

Jonah nodded, and she swore she saw a brief tight-lipped smile appear and vanish in an instant. "Alright. Looks like I'll see you then." He stepped out of his cubicle and left the office before they could exchange any other words.

• • •

The Golden Lantern was a popular Chinese restaurant that had been in the heart of the uptown Ruxlor community for decades. Both Rayne and Jonah had endless fond memories of both eating in and ordering and picking up food with their families, then going on their own for dates as they grew older. The place was so popular now that they had to build an extension of their parking lot and now had valet services. Jonah handed over the keys to his Wrangler after parking in front of the entrance so the valet driver could park for him. He headed inside and luckily was able to snag what he remembered was Rayne's favorite seat: a booth tucked away from the busier parts of the restaurant, right beside a massive fish tank. Nervous, he tugged on the collar of his creme-colored polo shirt and wiped his clammy hands on his pants. Why he was so anxious? He didn't have an answer.

Rayne appeared ten minutes later, out of her uniform and now dressed in a simple but flattering purple v-neck shirt, jeans, and ballet flats, her hair in a low ponytail, a few curls escaping. Jonah had to foolishly remind himself not to stare as he took a long sip of his ice water. A waitress appeared then and asked if they were ready to order, in which Jonah recited both his and her usual orders, drinks, and desserts.

"You remembered." Rayne said as the waitress took their menus and walked away. She looked into his eyes for a moment then broke their gaze.

"Of course. I could never forget." Jonah said with sincerity. "So, uh...how are your parents?"

"Pretty good. They're both back to work now."

"Oh, yeah, the book tour. Lacey got a copy of your mom's new book. She's a big fan and hopes she can sign it for her."

"Who?" she raised an eyebrow.

"My dad's new wife. You haven't met her yet."

"Oh..." Rayne averted her gaze down and clasped her hands together in her lap. "Tell him I said congratulations."

"I will." The small talk was killing him on the inside—what he wouldn't give to go back to their seemingly never-ending and intimate conversations about anything that'd come to their minds. He wondered if Rayne felt the same way. The discussion fell flat until their meals arrived, consisting of savory steaming hot bowls of lo mein noodles, sesame chicken, rice, vegetables, egg rolls, and crab rangoons. Red wine was poured into their glasses in the middle of the table. As they dug in, they began to talk about the case, and the awkwardness mostly melted away.

"We should go back to Brentwood's house and take a look through his office, and the place that he worked at." Rayne suggested.

"If we can somehow find evidence that Brentwood and Patrice Latimore were both working on this story somehow, that could bring us one step closer to finding out who did this." Jonah added, glad they were on the same page.

"Brentwood was a radio show host, wasn't he?" Rayne asked. "Maybe figuring out what he talked about on-air will be useful."

"He was a popular host, from the looks of it, but I doubt he would talk about serial killers on his morning shows, especially the one Latimore centered her story around. It wouldn't make sense."

She nodded slowly, no longer eating. "Do you...do you think there will be any more victims?"

Jonah wanted to lie, but he knew he couldn't fool Rayne; they had both studied the darkness and cruelties of the world. Although she was trying to remain hopeful, they both knew the answer. He looked out of the large windowpane beside them as a light rain began to fall. "Let's pray there's not."

They both knew one thing was for sure: this wouldn't stop until they found their culprit.

"Why were you so quick to pull out your gun back in Valencia?" she asked.

"Because you never know what's out there." Jonah said matter-of-factly.

"There wasn't a visible threat."

"No," he corrected, looking into her eyes with intention, "there wasn't a threat yet."

• • •

"I don't think going to the producer's office will do us any good." Owen said as he drove the Porsche down the dark main road that evening, going outbound. "We signed a contract."

Neevah was in the passenger seat, still visibly seething from their encounter with her sister the day before. The eerie night sky above them was onyx-black and starless. "I could care less about the contract, Owen. We still need to try."

"And when that doesn't work?"

A few moments of heavy silence passed. "Then we stick to our plan. When the press release for this project and Simone's book come out, we'll tell her everything. If she asks first. Until then, we don't say a word but try to keep abreast of the investigations without hovering over her. Hopefully, my sister's publisher drops the deal once they find out what's been happening."

"You'll tell Rayne everything, right?" Owen glanced at her.

Neevah took a shuddery breath in, then blew it out. "Yes. I will. Everything."

With their exit approaching, Owen flicked on his turn signal and merged into the far right lane. He lightly tapped the brake pedal, but the car didn't slow.

"There's no rush to get there, honey. I'm sorry if my nerves are making you feel like we have to get there as soon as possible." Neevah sighed. "They'll be filming something until ten, I think."

"No, it's not that. The brakes...they're not working."

"What?"

Owen stepped on the brakes with a little more force this time, but no luck. He stomped harder. Nothing. "This car is still fairly new, there's no way the brakes are shot already..." He paused and sniffed, inhaling sharply as they were approaching a curve in the road that led vehicles out of the highway. He looked around the inside of the car, confused. "Do you smell that...?" It smelled of burning rubber and exhaust fumes as they continued to accelerate faster.

"I don't know—" Neevah gasped, "—look out!"

Owen gripped the steering wheel and tried to swerve around the tree, but it was too late. They slammed into it, the car erupting in bright orange and red flames.

• • •

Bex's office phone rang loudly.

She decided to stay at the field office for part of the night shift, guzzling copious amounts of coffee as she wracked her brain sorting through digital case files on her desktop computer. She was simultaneously holding everything together regarding the new murders as well as old cases that were still assigned to her unit. She reached over her desk to answer the call. "Ruxlor City FBI, this is Agent Chapman." she said monotone as she tossed an empty styrofoam coffee cup into the trash can across the room.

"This is Monroe, Ruxlor City Chief of Police." Chief Monroe said. "We got another one."

8

BOTH ROOKIES' WORK PHONES BUZZED IN their pockets simultaneously, causing a wave of dread to silently wash over them. Exchanging hesitant looks, they had a feeling that they knew why they were being called at this hour.

The body count had risen. Rayne watched Jonah slowly retrieve his phone first, then she copied. They opened their text messages and read the same message:

McAllister Hwy / Pittsburgh exit
Vehicle fire
2 victims - still have pulses
Get there ASAP & shadow forensics crew

"We'll take my truck." Jonah stood and put on his jacket. "There's no need to take both of our cars to the scene."

There was no time to argue with that as Jonah slapped a hundred dollar bill down on the table and they abandoned the rest of their food. They swiftly headed out of the restaurant and walked across the parking lot to the valet booth to retrieve the keys to Jonah's Jeep, knowing time was of the essence. Jonah gave the valet driver a generous tip as well, not having time to sort through bills and change, and they climbed into the SUV. A strong wave of nostalgia then sadness coursed through Rayne as she fastened her seatbelt. She hadn't been in his car in years, and memories of the last time they were in it made her blush. She pushed those thoughts away, but little did she know that Jonah was struggling to keep the memories at bay, too. They peeled out of the parking lot and took the quickest route to McAllister Highway, which ran straight through the middle of Ruxlor County. It took about twenty minutes to arrive in the vicinity of the Pittsburgh exit where Bex had stated the incident took place. They could see the firetrucks, cop cars, and traffic control vehicles scattered around in the distance.

They slowed to a stop in front of a police officer that was redirecting traffic to the lane furthest to the left of the road. Jonah rolled down his window and flashed his FBI badge, and they were granted clearance. He spotted Bex's sedan and parked beside it, and the two of them got out.

The vehicle was almost completely destroyed. The sleek Porsche 718 Boxster was now barely recognizable. Before crossing the yellow police tape, Jonah and Rayne slipped on white latex gloves provided by Bex, who also handed them each a small flashlight to better illuminate the dark area. They crossed the threshold and were met by two officers, one of them the chief of police, and a firefighter.

"We were able to salvage the license plate," the firefighter said, "but not much else."

"The plate is perfect." Bex said. "We appreciate your help."

"Normally we don't call in the FBI to stuff like this right away." the Ruxlor City Chief of Police Tucker Monroe said glumly. "Let alone Violent Crimes, but considering the recent calls we made to you guys, and the assumption that I made looking at this mess, I thought it was necessary."

"What's your report?" Bex asked.

"The car lost control and swerved into the tree. The entire thing went up in flames instantly, from the bottom up. We've got a witness that strongly confirms this happening." The chief sighed. "Usually, when there's a vehicle malfunction, to my knowledge just the engine up front has the potential of having a minor explosion with heavy smoke coming out from underneath the hood. But as you can see, this seems to be more of an implosion from directly underneath the center of the car." He pointed over to the vehicle where Bex's forensics unit was already snapping photos and collecting tiny piece of evidence.

"Let's get to work." Bex ordered. "I'll interview the witnesses myself and get their info. Davenport, Winters, come up with an analysis and run it by Leigh, please."

But as they came up to the car and Rayne shone her flashlight onto its remains, she did a double-take and her breath hitched in her throat. It was undoubtedly a late-model Boxster. Only one person drove a Boxster in this town.

That person was her mother.

"Wait..." she said, more to herself than to the group as she leaned down and snatched up the dented license plate that was on the ground. When she read the plate numbers, she gasped and dropped it as if it were still burning. Her hands began to tremble, and her head spun, the edges of her vision blurring.

"Rayne?" Jonah slowly walked over to her after watching her drop the plate, but she wasn't listening. Her mind was telling her one thing, but her body was telling her something else. She dashed over to the car and started to pry open one of the doors when Jonah held her back. "Rayne, you're obstructing evidence. You can't go in there. What's gotten into you?"

"My mom..." she could barely let out a whisper. "T-This is my mom's car..."

"What? Rayne, are you positive?"

"Y-Yes! That's her license plate. And who else do you know has this kind of car? The two victims—they're my parents!"

He looked at the remains for a few moments, then realization hit him like a punch to the chest. He did remember her mother purchasing the car when they were adolescents. He'd been in it a few times, but that was over a decade ago. He swallowed the knot of dread that had formed in his throat and forced himself to keep a clear mind and to stay composed. He turned and took her by the shoulders.

"Alright. Wherever they took your parents to, we need to get you there now. My guess is Smithson East."

Rayne opened her mouth to respond, but no words came out. Her eyes averted from Jonah's worried gaze and back to the car. Looking at the singed sedan, she couldn't begin to fathom what kind of pain and suffering her parents had just experienced. She'd studied some equally gruesome cases in school and was never shaken about them, but this one was no doubt different. When it was someone you loved who was victimized, the utter shock and pain was insurmountable.

Leigh Crenshaw jogged over to the duo, wearing her FBI windbreaker and hat, and asked what was going on. Jonah informed her.

"Well, you certainly don't need to stay here, Winters. The chief informed me that they're being taken to Smithson East Hospital's trauma center. It's headed back in the direction of Ruxlor. We'll get you there in no time." But Rayne couldn't move. It felt like her feet were glued to the ground. Leigh was still talking, but it sounded far away, as if she was speaking underwater or through a thick glass window. "...We'll keep you in the loop on our findings, but you can no longer stay on these investigations. Detective Winters, do you hear me? Winters?"

Rayne's breathing turned shallow, her chest constricted, and she could hear her heart beating rapidly in her eardrums. A wave of nausea overtook her, and her vision blurred.

"*Rayne?*" It was Jonah's voice now, also sounding far away.

"*She's in shock; let her process this.*" It was Bex.

Before she could try to stop it, her knees buckled beneath her, and she collapsed.

• • •

"Rayne...Rayne, can you hear me?"

Her eyes fluttered open. When her vision refocused, she realized she was in Jonah's car again. He was driving slightly over the speed limit on the highway, going back in the direction of Ruxlor County.

"I'm taking you to Smithson." Jonah glanced at her then back at the long stretch of road in front of them.

She sniffled. "Thank you."

Jonah nodded, not saying anything else.

They arrived at the emergency room entrance fifteen minutes later. Jonah parked crookedly in a loading zone and flicked on his hazard lights, then escorted Rayne inside, holding her elbow in case she would faint again. They were told they'd have to wait a while before receiving any updates about Neevah and Owen, and Rayne could hardly handle the agony of sitting in the waiting room knowing nothing. Jonah handed a Violent Crimes Unit card to the receptionist, telling her to bring out a social worker right away, that this 'accident' was an urgent matter and they couldn't sit around for too long. The woman behind the desk nodded and picked up the phone beside her.

About five minutes later, a man in a gray suit came into the waiting room and walked up to the pair. Jonah stood first and shook hands with him.

"Detective Davenport." he introduced himself.

"Patrick Cunningham, from Social Services." the graying, middle-aged man stated. "Will this be your case?"

"Yes, sir." Although Jonah didn't get verbal confirmation from Bex that he would be working this case, he was confident that this would be put right alongside Evan Brentwood's and Patrice Latimore's, and that he would be a crucial part of the investigations.

"Alright. And you are?" Cunningham said as Rayne shakily stood up to shake his hand, looking her up and down.

"Detective Winters, criminal profiler from the same unit." she said quickly.

"This is Rayne Winters." Jonah explained. "Those two people that you guys just got are her parents. Do you need a report?"

Cunningham shook his head once. "We already took report from the medics."

"So you were made aware of the event that caused this?"

"Indeed...Why don't we have a talk in one of our counseling rooms, where it's more private?"

"Lead the way." Jonah nodded, glancing around at the mass of people in the packed waiting room. Cunningham turned and walked to a staff-only door, where he buzzed himself in using his ID badge. He led them down a corridor to a tiny room that was labeled 'FAMILY CONSULT.' It was a small space set up with two leather chairs and a couch, a coffee table, and a fish tank in one corner. Jonah and Rayne sat together on the larger couch. Cunningham took a seat in one of the single chairs facing them.

"I am sincerely sorry you are dealing with this, Detective Winters." he started. "I'll tell you both everything that the doctor has informed me of so far: Owen, the driver, has suffered third-degree burns along his arms and legs and some first-degree burns on his abdomen, and has a pretty significant concussion from the impact of the crash. He has a few broken bones and sprains that they are assessing now, but we're considering him lucky to have even survived an incident such as this one. He's sleeping right now under some heavy sedatives, so it's going to be quite a while before he wakes up. As for Neevah, who was in the passenger seat, they had to place her into a temporary medically induced coma to save her life; her body sustained more traumatic injuries, so that was the best plausible option."

"B-But, where are they? I need to see them." Rayne said.

"You both can see Owen in a few minutes when he is assigned a boarding room in our burn recovery unit, but I'll have to touch base with the doctor regarding Neevah; she just got out of surgery and is still in critical condition, and there are a lot of staff in the room with her right now."

Hearing this news crushed Rayne's spirits even more. She didn't know what was worse: seeing her mother's car smashed into the tree and registering that she and her father were the next victims, or hearing about how they've suffered. She rested her elbows on her knees and buried her face into the palms of her hands.

"We appreciate your help, Mr. Cunningham." Jonah said as he wrapped an arm around Rayne's shoulders, hoping he was at least somewhat a comforting presence to her.

"I'll go see what Mr. Winters's new room number is going to be and I'll get it right to you guys." Patrick Cunningham said, then he stood and left the room, slowly closing the door behind him.

After a few long moments, Jonah spoke. "It's alright, Rayne. Everything is going to be okay—"

"Everything is *not* going to be okay." Rayne said sharply, slinking away from his embrace and standing up. She crossed her arms over her chest. "This entire case just keeps spiraling and we can't control it. We have no suspects, no leads, no motive, hardly any evidence. Who is doing this?"

"If my mother's case taught me anything, it'd be to never lose hope. Ever." he said softly, also standing and putting his hands into the front pockets of his jacket. He blinked a few times, not daring letting himself become emotional. That would only cause his tough exterior to crack, and he had to be strong. For himself. For her. "It's been four years and we haven't found her killer. Yet. But we're close, I can feel it. We may not have the upper hand right now, but the case will not go cold. As long as you believe everything will work out, then it'll work out. This is no different."

Rayne sighed, averting her gaze to the ground as a wave of guilt coursed through her. "I...I'm sorry. I'm not mad at you, I'm mad at whoever did this to my mother and father. They didn't deserve this..."

Jonah entwined his hands with hers, and she looked back up at him with tearful eyes. "The squad and I are going to do everything in our power to catch this person and bring them to justice. You can count on it."

"Jonah, I'm counting on myself, too; I'm staying on this case." she said with finality.

He visibly paused for just a moment. "Are you sure?"

"Yes. I'm not going to rest until my parents get the justice they deserve, and the other victims."

Jonah didn't say anything else after that, instead he pulled her into a tight embrace, trying to stop himself from thinking the worst: if Rayne's parents were targeted and supposed to be dead, did that mean she could be next?

9

BEX YAWNED LOUDLY AS SHE USED her ID badge to unlock the frosted glass door that led to the Violent Crimes division of the FBI field office. She took a few steps to go to her office, but when she saw movement in her peripheral vision, coming from the computer lab, she froze. It was dark with few lights on in this part of the building; it was four o'clock in the morning and faculty didn't start coming in until about six. On occasion Bex liked to come in extra early to work on cases on her own and prepare notes for the morning briefings, then leave earlier in the afternoon. She waited for more movement, but there was none.

On high alert, she withdrew her .25 handgun from her back pocket with one hand expertly, took it off of safety, and waited a few moments before she barged into the lab, aiming at the shadowy figure in the room.

"Whoa—Winters?" Bex said, flabbergasted as she secured her gun back on safety mode and pocketed it discreetly, then flipped on the lightswitch, illuminating the large room. "What are you doing here at this hour?"

"I'm sorry, Chief, but I won't be long. I'm just...trying to connect the dots here; some of this just isn't making any sense." The exhaustion in Rayne's voice was apparent as she tried to tidy up the space she was occupying. There was an array of files and notes scattered around the desk.

"You don't need to be here, Winters. It's been less than twenty-four hours since your parents' crash. I'm dismissing you from these cases, effective immediately."

Rayne's head snapped up to look at Bex across the room, stunned. "What? No, that won't be necessary. I can help—we just need a new lead, that's all..."

Bex held up a hand to stop her. "I've experienced firsthand how one's emotions can negatively affect an assignment. Even put an entire team in danger because their choices were influenced by their heart and not their brain and calculation. Their judgment was clouded, adding more room for error. That is not what we want right now."

Rayne, silent, couldn't find words to say to combat Bex's response. It was because she knew her boss was right; she'd learned this not only in FBI training down at Quantico but in school as well, one wrong decision could prove detrimental, even cost lives. But it didn't deter her from walking away completely. She couldn't simply step down, not while her own parents were currently fighting for their lives due to an act of terror.

"I'm hunting down who did this, with or without you and the team. They will pay for this, one way or another." Rayne said in a low tone, and left the lab. She became more infuriated as she walked through the halls of the field office and out the doors to the parking lot, feeling numb and utterly helpless. She could barely keep her thoughts straight, but she wasn't going to stop until justice was secured. There was an assailant walking free, coming too close to robbing her of her family, and she was seeing red. They weren't supposed to survive. Did the killer know they had lived? Why were they targets in the first place? Was there something she didn't know about, something that was being kept from her?

She was not going to rest until she found out.

• • •

That Saturday morning, a few days after being called to the scene where Neevah and Owen Winters had crashed, Jonah cradled his cell phone in his hands, staring down at the black screen. He had called Rayne about a dozen times over the course of the weekend, only to be sent straight to voicemail each time. He didn't see her at work on Friday, which made him grow more concerned. She told him at the hospital that she was still committed to the cases, but had she changed her mind? It was gnawing away at his conscience, not knowing where she was and if she was okay. He knew what it felt like to lose a parent so suddenly. Although the Winters were still alive, they both remained in critical condition and things could still very well take a turn for the worst.

He sat inside of a locally owned café in downtown Ruxlor City, trying to put his mind at ease as he pocketed his phone and picked up the bagel breakfast sandwich he'd ordered, which was now cold. After looking at it for a few seconds, he put it back down on the plate. He hadn't had an appetite since appearing on what was now a crime scene and watching the pure horror and shock register on Rayne's face. He knew that feeling all too well, how the world seemed to slow down and freeze around you, the way all oxygen suddenly left your lungs and constricted your chest, the way your body slowly betrayed you as it began to shut down, and you couldn't control any of it. Then came the rage—the anger, bargaining, depression, then acceptance. If you did not know how to navigate it, grief could be a dangerous thing to battle, especially alone.

His nerves were shot, but he dialed her phone number once more, silently pleading for her to pick up. He held the phone up to his ear, listening to it ring. He waited.

Then silence.

He heard light, shallow breathing on the other end of the line and knew that she'd answered, but she didn't say anything for a moment. "What's up?"

"I would just like to know where you're at, that's all."

In her condo on the other side of town, Rayne sat on the floor in her bedroom with her back against the wall, eyelids heavy from lack of sleep, laptop open in front of her. She combed through her curls with her fingers, contemplating. "I'm at home."

"Are you okay? I haven't heard anything from you and haven't seen you at headquarters, so I was starting to get kinda worried. I'm sorry if I'm being a little overbearing."

"I understand and it's fine, Jo. You're not overbearing. Bex kicked me off the case, so that's why I didn't show up to work yesterday. She didn't tell you guys?"

"She said you were taking some time off to be with your parents, but she didn't say you were off the assignment entirely. I heard her and Leigh bring up your name in a conversation in the breakroom, but I didn't want to be seen eavesdropping so I let it be."

Rayne let out a long sigh over the phone. She didn't know why she would be a topic of conversation, let alone amongst her coworkers, but she told herself not to ponder about it. "Well, has any progress been made? Maybe that's why they're talking about me?" Maybe Bex changed her mind and will put me back on the case, she thought hopefully.

"Unfortunately no, but whatever happens I'll let you know as soon as possible."

"I appreciate that, Jonah. Thank you."

"Anytime...Have you eaten yet? I can bring takeout and we can go over notes together, if you're up for it. I just need to see that you're okay or else I don't really believe you. I know this is an emotional time for you and I know this is a lot to take in, and it's not good for you to be completely isolated right now. Trust me, I know how it feels."

"Hm." she hummed. She couldn't pass up the offer; she hadn't eaten much over the last two days and couldn't really muster up the energy to get up and cook a meal right now. Plus, they could continue discussing the investigations together since she wasn't allowed back at the field office until they had a suspect in custody and closed the case for good. Another thing, she could finally force herself to come clean to Jonah give him the apology he'd needed to hear years ago. They both needed a clean slate, especially now, and this was the perfect time to do so. "I'll send you the address."

Jonah inaudibly sighed a breath of relief. "Give me about an hour and I'll be there."

"Okay." Rayne hung up then rubbed her eyes with the palms of her hands. She didn't want company, not right now, but she knew Jonah was right. Besides, she was growing paranoid being alone within these walls, and paranoia was the last thing she needed while dealing with a case like this.

• • •

1015 Dove Lane, Unit 40.

Leaving the café that was now getting more crowded by the hour, Jonah headed to his SUV that was parked on the street, paid the parking meter, and climbed inside. He bluetoothed his cell phone to his car's media system and pulled up the address Rayne had texted to him on the touchscreen's navigation display. It told him he was twenty minutes away from the complex she lived in with heavy traffic, so on a good day he concluded about ten or fifteen minutes. He called Golden Lantern and ordered their usual meals to-go, then he was on his way.

• • •

Rayne realized that she actually needed to get up and make it look like she hadn't been wallowing around like a zombie for the last forty-eight hours.

Granted, she knew Jonah probably wouldn't care about how she looked at this point—considering both of her parents were in the intensive care unit at the hands of a criminal—but for a reason she didn't quite know, she still wanted to put a small amount of effort into her appearance and make herself look slightly less frazzled. After hanging up the phone, she scrambled to get in the shower, standing under steaming hot water for about ten minutes as an attempt to help relax her muscles and wash the tension from her body, dressed in a low-necked white knit romper, pinned her hair into a messy low bun, and rummaged through her moving boxes that she had yet to unpack to retrieve a bottle of vanilla and rose-scented perfume and lotion. She added simple gold earrings with a matching bracelet set, splashed her face with water in her bathroom sink to further wake herself up, then applied lipgloss. But her eyes, the supposed gateway to the soul, were still tired and dejected. It was the only thing she couldn't hide.

As if on cue, at seven o'clock sharp, she heard her cell phone go off with a text alert. She found her phone abandoned on the bedroom floor, and she picked up to open the message. It was from Jonah.

Jonah: **Tall black gate on Canobie Boulevard?**

She swiftly texted back: **Yes. I'll buzz you in.**

There was a security guard at the front gate 24/7, and she got text alerts sent right to her phone every time she had a visitor, asking her permission for them to either let the visitor into the complex or turn them away. She gave the guard the greenlight to let Jonah through. During the agonizingly long five minutes it took him to find a parking spot and find her condominium, she tidied up her home the best that she could and looked at herself in the mirror umpteen times before the doorbell rang.

Suddenly, her stomach tied up in knots, and she had wished she'd declined his offer to come.

But, she walked over to the door anyway. She squinted through the peephole out of paranoia, resulting in her heart fluttering in her chest, and she opened the door.

She looked up at him blankly, suddenly not knowing what to say.

"Hey." Jonah spoke first with a soft smile. "Uh, is it alright if I come in?"

"Oh, sorry. Of course." She opened the door wider, and he stepped into the foyer as she swiftly locked it behind them. Even though she knew well enough that the chances of their perpetrator being within the walls of the gated living community were very slim, she couldn't help it as the paranoia crept into her mind. She closed her eyes, her hand still lingering on the doorknob, trying to stop her brain from spiraling and thinking any more bad thoughts. *It's safe here,* she thought. *At least, I can only hope.*

Before she could open her eyes, she felt strong arms pulling her into a tight embrace, and the words, "I'm sorry." A wave of shock hit her first, but it quickly dissolved as she returned the embrace, wrapping her arms around his larger frame and taking a deep breath in, taking in an all too familiar scent that she'd never forgotten.

"You don't need to say sorry." Rayne sniffled. "If anyone needs to apologize, it should be me." She began to feel all of the emotions that she had tried to suppress bubbling back up again, tears threatening to spill from her eyes. "This isn't your fault."

"And it's not yours either." Jonah pulled back, leaving two firm hands on her shoulders. "You're already dealing with enough as it is right now, and dwelling on the past isn't going to help us, is it? You need to let the past go, Rayne. You did what was best for you, and I did what was best for me. I'm being completely honest when I say everything is going to be okay."

"But..." She couldn't find the words to combat what he had just said, simply because she was still in a state of denial. She was in the wrong. She was the one who left without looking back, despite her best friend's world being ripped apart. He needed her back then, and she had completely disappeared from his life. Now the tables were turned. *I don't deserve this. I don't deserve his empathy or unwavering support at all.*

"No but's." Jonah interjected. He held out a small bouquet of a half of a dozen red roses between them. "I stopped by the market on my here and got these. I thought they'd brighten up your new space."

Rayne accepted them graciously but forced herself not to tear up at the simple but kind gesture. "You really didn't have to. These look beautiful. Thank you."

"It's the least I could do." he shrugged with a soft smile as he set the heavy paper bag full of Chinese food down on the kitchen countertop. He took off his FBI windbreaker and draped it over a barstool, then proceeded to empty the bag, pulling out hot containers that were packed with their favorite savory dishes, plastic utensils, and napkins. While he did this, Rayne filled up a vacant vase with water, trimmed the roses' ends, and placed them into the vase.

They devoured their dinner in silence on the living room couch, the flat screen television on the local news station in front of them, but Jonah didn't mind the quietness. He knew Rayne probably had a million thoughts running through her head at the moment, so he gave her some necessary space while they ate. His father Sam Davenport messaged him then, asking if he was going to make it home for dinner tonight, and they exchanged a short text conversation before he shut down his cell phone and pocketed it, wanting to nonverbally let Rayne know that she had his full, undivided attention. However, his work phone was still on, as was hers. Updates for a case could come sporadically, a new lead could open up, a new piece of evidence could be found, and Bex wanted her agents informed as soon as possible whenever that happened.

Jonah just hoped he wouldn't get called onto another crime scene tonight.

Reporters and journalists around the area were still obsessing over the fiery murders—both attempted and finished. The TV showed a reporter standing on the side of McAllister Highway, close to the remains of the fire. She was stating details about Neevah and Owen's car crash and interviewing witnesses. She did not reveal their names directly, but indicated that there was a male and female rushed to an undisclosed hospital, and that this marked the third bizarre fire in the county alone for the week. But this was to be expected; two people were dead, and Ruxlor City wasn't known for having multiple fires such as these, especially in the fall. The city was in an apparent frenzy, and that only put more pressure on Bex and the team to get justice.

"Any leads open up today, for any of our cases?" Rayne asked.

Jonah shook his head. "Unfortunately, no."

"Did any fingerprints come back from the medical examiner?"

He shook his head again. "We didn't get any prints from Brentwood's house, or Latimer's, or your mother's car. Whoever planted the flammables and explosives was gloved, or they wiped everything down beforehand. But we did learn that our first two victims showed signs of being in a struggle, so we think they had pretty violent altercations with the arsonist before their deaths."

Rayne nodded slowly. "Maybe they were trying to pry information from them before killing them? Evan Brentwood was a radio host but also had other private business ventures, and Patrice Latimore's work computer was reported missing from her job. I wonder if either of them had valuable information that our suspect didn't want anyone else to know about."

"That's possible. If only any witnesses came forward, that would help."

"No one's talked yet?"

"Not one person."

"People must really be scared."

"With someone like this on the loose," Jonah said, "I would be too."

10

"WE SHOULD BRING IN RAYNE FOR questioning." Agent Leigh Crenshaw stated. "Not right now, but after we finish the rest of the interrogations today..."

"I have to agree with you." Bex replied, pacing around the small conference room after the Criminal Profiling Unit's daily agenda meeting had concluded and everyone else had left. "Not just one, but both of her parents were targeted by an unknown arsonist and left for dead—potentially the same one who killed Brentwood and Latimore. Maybe she has some useful info that can help us narrow down our suspect list, and we can talk to relatives and friends. We need to find who has strong ties to the Winters, and who would have the capability of pulling off something like this."

Agent Roscoe Hall stepped into the room just then, holding up a thin manila file folder. "Neevah Alistair-Winters is a pretty interesting woman." he handed the file over to Bex, who opened it and flipped through the pages, Leigh looking over her shoulder. "She's a true crime writer under her maiden name and has made quite a name for herself. She's got a ton of awards and recognitions and millions of fans. Looks like she travels all over for speaking engagements and conferences. I also learned from her website that she actually meets with victims and their families personally and does her own private research when writing her books. Her last book was published in 2020 by a Big Five publishing house, but it doesn't take place here, or in this country at all, matter-of-fact. But it's sold almost a half a million copies since then, and another publishing deal has been reported for a new book next year. A lot of the crimes she writes about are pretty fascinating."

"This is interesting information, but can any of the things she wrote about motivate someone to try and kill her?" Leigh asked. "And if so, where does that leave our last two victims? If this were a personal vendetta, she would be the only one."

"That is true," Bex said, "but it won't hurt to try to get some more background on Mrs. Winters and her success. Find some people we can bring in to question ASAP. I'll go finish dealing with Mr. Brentwood's case; we finished going through his suspect list this morning, and since no witnesses have come forward and we don't have any camera footage of the fire or a crime being committed, unfortunately we have to shelve his case for now so I can release his body to Lana so she can make his funeral arrangements."

"Maybe," Roscoe Hall said, "we'll be more lucky with Ms. Latimore's case; we got two witnesses now that both said they saw a verbal and physical altercation between her and an unknown man just a half an hour before a fire was reported. Maybe that suspect will match up with whoever started the fire that killed Brentwood, and we'll get two birds with one stone."

• • •

Angelo Maguire, a fiftysomething bestselling mystery novelist, was first up that morning. He sat awkwardly at the steel table in one of the interrogation rooms, fiddling with his fingers and biting his lip nervously. He looked well for his age, with no grays in his thick brown hair, olive-toned skin, and chiseled facial structure. He wore black dress pants with a matching blazer and brown shirt underneath.

Leigh stepped into the room and closed the door behind her, then took a seat across from him, sitting casually with one leg crossed over the other, clicking a ballpoint pen with her thumb. But Angelo's body didn't loosen up.

"So, you are Mr. Angelo Maguire." Leigh stated.

"Y-Yes, ma'am. That is me." Angelo cleared his throat and tugged on his shirt. He had a deep baritone voice but it was cracking under pressure. What pressure, Leigh didn't quite know. All she was doing was sitting here, looking him in the eye. She had a feeling he wasn't guilty, but proceeded anyway.

"How did you and Neevah meet?" she asked simply.

"Well, we met at a writers conference in San Francisco over two decades ago, our editors introduced us to each other. I bought her a drink, we chatted for a bit, went to some of the workshops and seminars together, then swapped email addresses. Soon enough, we came up with the idea to write a fiction series together after readers saw pics of us at the event and demanded we write something together. Our agents put the deal together and it became a hit."

"Would you say this sparked into a friendship between the two of you?"

"I would say so, yes. Although it was strictly professional due to our rigorous publishing deadlines, we did grow closer when writing together. I'd definitely call her a friend."

"Have you kept in contact with her since the series came out?"

He sighed. "No...not really. We went on these industry-led writing retreats together, but she met her husband a year later and we were only able to talk at events and release parties and whatnot. We chatted via email a couple times a year, but that was only to say 'Happy birthday' or 'Happy New Year.' The conversations dwindled after that."

"Have you always lived in Ruxlor?"

"I did grow up in the county, yes. Blue Valley, to be exact. But I moved to New York City for a few months after our publisher canceled the last book in our series. I branched off and started new projects there. Then I lived in Hawai'i up until now."

"And what brings you back here, of all places? At this time?"

Angelo shrugged. "Inherited my uncle's home in Venzor. I took a teaching position at Ruxlor University but still write full time. My family is going through a rough time so I came back home to support them. I still have my property in Honolulu, but I don't know when I'll be going back."

"When did you move back to Ruxlor?"

"A couple days ago—Sunday the first of October was when I caught my last flight to the Pittsburgh International

Airport. I had a few things I had to get settled back in Honolulu."

"Have you seen Neevah at all last week?" Leigh was jotting everything down in her notepad.

"I ran into her at the pizza place we frequently order from and we talked for a good twenty minutes. She did seem frazzled and disoriented, though, but I have a feeling that it wasn't from my presence. It seemed like something was bothering her, like she was worried about something. She looked really paranoid."

"Did she confide in you as to what was going on?"

"No. I let her know that she could tell me, that I wouldn't go blabbing to anyone about our conversation, but she insisted that she didn't want to involve me in it. I gave her my new phone number and said if she needed anything at all to contact me. Then we went our separate ways."

"I see...Have you ever had any intimate encounters with her from the time you met up until last week?"

Angelo held back a chuckle and shook his head. "If you must know, Detective, we did share one night of uninterrupted bliss...in 1998. Before we parted ways and before she got married, might I add. What are you implying?"

Leigh ignored this. "What were you doing on the evening of Thursday, October fifth? Approximately eleven-thirty p.m.?"

Angelo didn't need much time to think about that. "I was at my sister and her husband's house in uptown. I was still determining if I wanted to move into our uncle's house or get a place elsewhere. I have our text history to prove it, and she has cameras around her house if you need to see that I was there...What happened at that specific time? Is Neevah alright?"

"To put it simply: her car exploded. But not just any explosion; we think it was the work of a serial arsonist. She wasn't the first victim."

Angelo gulped audibly. He could barely utter the words. "Is...is she alive?"

"Critical, but alive, yes."

"Goodness, that's awful. I wish I could do something to help. I don't think prodding into my personal life did much for you." he tried to smile, but a wave of worry washed over his face.

"No worries. Thank you for your time, Mr. Maguire. I'll keep in touch." Leigh handed him the business card with the contact information to the FBI Field Office. "If you remember anything about your encounter with Mrs. Winters last week, or remember any details about what she told you, please call this number as soon as you can."

She then signaled her hand at the one-way tempered glass window where she knew an agent was standing, and he came in at her command to escort Mr. Maguire out of the building.

His alibi was strong; public records along with his social media pages proved that he was living in Hawai'i for the last twenty years. He also just finished an east coast book tour a short time before coming back to Ruxlor (Leigh had learned this after skimming through his website this morning, as well as reading headlines of both himself and Neevah as what critics called a 'powerhouse writing duo'). He was nowhere near the city at the time of the incident, and in Leigh's opinion, did not have a viable motive to commit such an act.

Not wasting any time, she scratched his name off of her list and called for an agent to send in the next person.

• • •

That afternoon, Simone Alistair drummed her long, sangria-red fingernails on the steel table in the chilly interrogation room, visibly annoyed.

She stared back at her elegant and sophisticated appearance in the one-way mirror with a subtle smile, pleased with how she looked. No, she loved how she looked. She wore a chocolate-brown Fendi bodycon dress with black, knee-high heeled boots, her wavy black hair cascading down her back. Her face was lightly made up with foundation, blush, silver shimmering eyeshadow, and wine-purple colored matte lipstick. Even though she was in a dim, cold room with no windows at an FBI site, she never dared step outside looking anything short of glamorous. Her reputation (and ego, perhaps) never allowed anything less than perfection.

Sitting at her cubicle, Leigh skimmed through the information she'd acquired about their next suspect. Bex loomed over her shoulder.

"Look at this." Leigh pulled up a web page on her computer monitor, showing a professional headshot of a beaming Simone with another photo beside it of a section of an article copied from another website. "This is interesting."

"This could make her our prime suspect," Bex stated, "if we find any evidence, of course."

Moments later, Leigh entered the interrogation room where Simone sat. "Good afternoon," she said as she sat down in her chair and placed her notepad on the table in front of her. "You must be Ms. Alistair."

"The one and only, yes. How long is this going to take?" Simone demanded.

"You are aware that your sister is in a coma, right? We believe that her and her husband along with two other deceased victims were targeted. We're just trying to figure out who did it and why."

Simone broke eye contact then, looking over to the wall on her right. "Yes, I've been told." She sighed and crossed her arms over her stomach. "I'm supposed to be visiting my sister tonight with my niece, Rayne. Is she here?"

"I'm not sure." Leigh lied. She wasn't allowed to discuss the whereabouts of her colleagues, even if they were currently on a hiatus like Rayne Winters was. "What were you doing on the night of Thursday, October fifth at approximately eleven-thirty p.m.?"

"Well, I was sitting at home with my fiancé when Rayne called me sometime after midnight and broke the news to us."

"And what did you do then?"

"Nothing, really...I told her to stay calm and to keep me updated."

"You didn't go to the hospital?"

Simone shrugged. "It wouldn't have made a difference; Rayne told me they were in critical condition and no one was permitted to see them yet anyway. To my knowledge, they're admitted now so I'm able to go see them."

"Alright. Tell me about this." Leigh took out a printout of a web page screenshot from her manila folder and slid it across the table for Simone to see, who glanced down at it and chuckled lightly.

"You think my book deal has something to do with their accident?"

Leigh could tell Simone was trying to save face and act indifferent towards the situation, but she knew she wasn't trying to say much for a reason. That meant she was no doubt hiding something. Leigh pressed her pointer finger down onto the photograph with emphasis. "What exactly is this book about? No title yet, but the subtitle says Surviving the Humble Creek Killer. Explain that to me."

"Well...it tells the story of how my family and I got in the crosshairs of a serial stalker turned killer. It also gives some insight of my upbringing—what my wonderful life was like before it was ripped apart, before my family knew we had a close relationship with a criminal. But somehow, people were drawn to our story. Almost obsessed. Soon, people started asking us to speak about it, tell them how we coped, how we were able to move on with our lives. My family rejected everything and isolated themselves from our town, but I decided to start speaking up about our experience. That's how I was able to jumpstart my career as a motivational speaker, mentor, life coach. I have dedicated fans everywhere now. That tragedy changed the entire trajectory of my life for the better."

"But not for Neevah."

"No...I guess not." Simone looked down.

"And how do you think this correlates to why you're sitting here right now, talking to me, an FBI agent?"

Simone drew in a shuddery breath. She didn't respond for a long while. "Because, he...he almost killed her."

11

"SHE'S NOT ENTIRELY OFF THE HOOK yet." Special Agent Leigh Crenshaw dropped the file and let it fall onto Bex's desk with a soft thud later that evening. "She was apprehensive about telling me about her memoir even though the deal has been made public—and she confessed that Neevah Winters had an encounter with a murderer before. I don't want to make an arrest today, but what else could she be hiding that could be crucial to helping us solve this?"

Bex skimmed over the publishing deal report that was screenshotted and printed out from Neevah Alistair's website. The report didn't say much, but from what Leigh had briefed to her after the interrogation, it didn't need one; Simone already had thousands of fans from the career she'd built off of her family's tragedy, and they already knew what exactly it would be about. What surprised Bex the most wasn't the memoir itself, but Neevah Winters's close encounter with a serial stalker. That small piece of information had turned their entire case upside down. Were they dealing with a personal vendetta? Someone bent on finishing the job that they had failed to complete years ago? If so, how were the first two victims connected to all of this?

"We'll bring the team together in the morning and you can show them the video footage of your interview with Ms. Alistair." Bex said. It was getting late and nearing the end of their shift, so Bex added the file of papers pertaining to Simone to their folder that was dedicated to their arson cases and stood from her desk. Leigh followed her to the break room where they clocked out. "I'll have Anisa and Keon dig up her phone call history to see if it matches up to what she told you."

"We should still question Rayne tomorrow." Leigh added.

"Bring her in first thing in the morning." Bex replied and walked out the door.

• • •

When Simone was back in her Audi Q8, enjoying the heated seats and soothing jazz music on her way to her niece's apartment, she was happy to be out of that cold, dingy interrogation room but annoyed at the fact that she could potentially be called back in for more questioning. What else did they need to know? She wasn't there when Neevah crashed her car, she was sitting at home with her fiancé and she could prove that. She knew this all was for her sister's sake and the sake of her brother-in-law, but did these people really think she could have pulled that off? Did she look like the deranged arsonist that terrorized her family decades ago?

She wanted to ask the agent if there were any outstanding clues at any of the crime scenes. The sensationalized 'Humble Creek Killer' had never left any traces of evidence behind at any of his crime scenes, resulting in all of the homicide cases that were allegedly completed by him leading to dead ends and being dropped after eventually crimes that matched his terrorizing style stopped. The Alistairs were the last to witness his wrath.

Until now.

Was this his way of getting revenge? Was he back to get her?

No, don't think like that. Everything is fine! Simone mentally yelled at herself as she entered the Canobie Commons gated living community with the passcode she was given prior and parked outside of Rayne's building, although she could feel deep down inside that something wasn't right. Evan Brentwood, the documentary's leading producer, and

Patrice Latimore, one of their script writers, were dead—burned alive from an unknown cause. Just the way the Humble Creek Killer had claimed his victims...

But she wasn't afraid. No one was going to rattle her or try to take away everything she had made for herself since telling her family's story—not even the man who'd started all of this havoc himself.

The passenger door swung open, and she flinched. But when she saw that it was just Rayne, she gave a flashy smile and waited for her to fasten her seatbelt before putting the SUV back into Drive and leaving the complex. "Hey, hun!" she glanced at her niece before averting her eyes back onto the road. Simone could tell she hadn't gotten a full night's rest in a while. "So, how long have you been with the FBI branch here? I thought you were staying down in Virginia?"

"Not long." Rayne shrugged dejectedly.

Simone pursed her lips, not knowing what else to add to the already dying conversation. "I didn't see your car in the parking lot. You still got your father's old BMW?"

"I do, it still runs great. I, uh, I'm actually on temporary leave until this case is solved. My boss thinks my emotions will get in the way of our work." Rayne mumbled the last part.

"Oh." Simone sighed. "I am terribly sorry to hear that, hun. Everything will work out, I know it. We just have to stay positive, you know?"

Neither of them said anything else. About twenty minutes later they were approaching the vast, modern campus of Smithson East Hospital on the eastern side of the town. Tension filled the car, making the air seemingly thick. Simone drove up to the valet drivers, and they exited the car and made their way to the main entrance. Once inside, they were cleared by security and stopped at a receptionist's desk in the lobby.

"Hello, miss, we're here to see Neevah and Owen Winters." Simone gave a dazzling smile to the young woman behind the desk.

After a few moments of typing at a computer, the receptionist looked up and said, "Sorry, we don't have anyone here under those names."

"B-But, I know—"

"5-7-5-9." Rayne interjected. The receptionist nodded and began typing again. She saw her aunt's quizzical look and added, "Extra security measures. This is being treated as an attempted double homicide, and no one can see my parents without giving the access code. Remember that number." Simone nodded silently.

"You two are good to go up. They actually just got moved to joint rooms within the burn recovery unit: rooms 8011 and 8012 on the eighth floor. I'll let them know you're on the way."

"Thank you, ma'am." Rayne replied, and Simone followed her past the receptionist's desk and to a pair of elevators. One dinged and opened its doors, and they stepped inside. Rayne pressed the 8 button, and they descended upward. It was an awkwardly silent trip, neither one of them saying anything to each other.

Moments later they arrived on the eighth floor, and proceeded to the room numbers the receptionist had told them to go to. Rayne paused just outside of her mother's door, and Simone placed a reassuring hand on her shoulder.

"It's all right, hun." she said confidently. "We'll go in together, okay?"

Rayne nodded as her aunt slowly opened the door.

As they entered the intensive care room that was well illuminated by two windowpanes of golden rays of sunshine, Rayne vowed that she would find who did this to her mother, and that they would pay.

12

RAYNE PARKED IN THE EMPTY REAR parking lot that wasn't used often by staff, and slowly stepped out of her car. She locked it from the inside and closed the door slowly so she wouldn't have the use her keys and make any unneeded noise, then scanned the lot as she briskly walked up to a side entrance and buzzed herself in with her identification badge. She walked down the dim corridors to the Violent Crimes Unit, granted herself access, and proceeded through the suite towards her cubicle.

It was just past five o'clock that Sunday morning. She knew no one was going to be here on the weekend despite the major case they were dealing with, which would work in her favor. Bex did remove her from the investigation, but here she was, intending on doing a bit more research in their databases before gathering her notes and going back home. She didn't want to be on Bex's bad side, however, or tarnish her trust and become an agent who didn't follow their commander's orders faithfully without question, so this was the only time she could come and work on finding her parents' assailant. She simply couldn't help it. Did Bex really think she was just going to sit around while the killer walked free?

She flicked on a light switch that illuminated half of the office and walked over to her desk. But as she sat down, she realized...

Everything was gone.

"No, no—this can't be right." She opened all of her desk drawers and file cabinets to see that everything was still in their rightful places.

Except for her files regarding the arson case...

She frantically continued to search, but there was no luck. The files weren't anywhere. Stunned, she quickly retrieved her phone from her jacket pocket and dialed Jonah's number, hoping he would know something that would explain this. *Who would have taken them?* she thought. *And why?*

He picked up on the third ring. "Detective Davenport," she heard a stifled yawn on the other end of the line. "Ruxlor City FBI."

"Jonah," Rayne tried to keep her voice barely above a whisper, even though she knew she was the only one there.

"It's me. My papers from the case...they're all gone." she said breathlessly. "I handwrote most of my observations in a yellow notebook since we were hired, but I can't find it anywhere. All of my own files that had my research in them are gone too."

In his home, Jonah became fully awake almost instantly, jolting upright in his bed and rubbing his eyes. "Rayne? Why are you at the office? Are you alone?"

She ignored his questions. "Have you seen them at all recently? Those are the only copies I have."

"I did see your yellow notebook before I left my desk Friday afternoon. I can have someone from security playback the camera footage to see where they could've went. But, you really shouldn't be over there alone, especially when you're not on the assignment anymore. Is any night staff there?"

"I don't think we have night staff, it's completely vacant here."

"Okay, then turn around and go back home. There are still a lot of things up in the air, and none of us can afford to expose ourselves to any potential danger."

"Okay. I will." She hung up then, not knowing what else to say. He was the first person that'd come to her mind to call in her moment of panic, but now she instantly felt bad for bothering him at this time of day. Perhaps she was still guilty; she knew he had his own issues going on on top of the case, including his own mother's unsolved murder, and now she was simply burdening him more with her lack of thinking. He was right. She should have never came to the field office alone, even for a simple task of picking up her files. She forced herself to clear her head as she looked around the office space one last time before shutting off the lights, giving up. She headed back outside to her car that sat by itself in the dim lot, flustered, sleep deprived, and feeling utterly helpless.

She was the only one on the dark main road that she oftentimes took as a backway to get to the apartment complex faster. She drove past older bungalow and ranch style homes, small businesses, markets, and run down gas stations, a dozen questions swirling around in her mind.

Suddenly a pair of high beams illuminated her rearview and side mirrors, and she squinted, trying to see what was behind her. The blinding lights were closing in on her, and fast. She was already pushing forty-five MPH, as the speed limit was only forty, but the vehicle behind her showed no signs of slowing down. Annoyed, she slowly accelerated to fifty MPH, but it was no help. If she didn't go faster, she would be rear-ended. Rayne cursed under her breath as she looked for somewhere to turn onto, finding a residential road ahead. She sped up to try to put some distance between herself and the car behind her, then made a sharp right turn and continued her drive.

Moments later, someone turned onto the road behind her as well, and the high beamed lights returned, blinding her.

"What...?" she said to herself as she swiveled her head behind her, but she couldn't identify the car, let alone its reckless driver in the darkness of the night. Whoever they were, they were gaining on her again, fast. She honked her horn twice, but it didn't deter the driver one bit. The bigger vehicle, an SUV if Rayne had to guess, bumped the back of her sedan, causing it to jerk violently, and she lost her grip on the steering wheel. Luckily, she quickly regained control and sped up, but the other car stayed right on her tail.

It bumped her car again as they were approaching a bend in the road, this time much more roughly, causing Rayne to nearly spin out of control. She tried to steer her car back within the lines on their side of the road, but now the two vehicles were connected, and the larger car behind her was now pushing her car, almost controlling its direction.

It was pushing her towards the river.

No! She blared her horn again, desperate to tell the driver to stop, but deep down inside she knew it was no use. The bend in the road was becoming sharper, and she only had a fraction of a second to think...

She swerved then slammed on her brakes with a shrill scream, rolling down the hill and missing the embankment by mere inches.

PART THREE

13

THE BRIEFING WAS JUST CONCLUDING WHEN Rayne burst into the conference room the next morning.

"Bex, I need to talk to you." Rayne said breathlessly. "I was just—"

"Winters, what are you doing here?" Bex cut her off. The other agents glanced over at Rayne for a few seconds, then continued packing up their things to move to their designated workspaces for the remainder of the day. "You are not on this case anymore."

"Please, Chief. It's urgent."

Everyone walked past Rayne and filed out of the room, except for Bex and Leigh. And Jonah, who stayed seated at the roundtable. He cast a worried glance at Rayne, wondering what she was about to inform them.

"Whatever it is, it could be beneficial." Jonah said, closing his laptop and folding his hands together.

Bex sighed. "Okay, then. What is it?"

Rayne was going to speak, but suddenly her mouth went dry, her hands clammy, and her mind went blank trying to put the pieces of her story together. The events that had occurred last night were terrifyingly real and could have no doubt cost her life, but now, as she was putting the words together in her head, she wondered. *Will they believe my story?* There was no camera footage on the road she was on, and she didn't catch the driver or the license plate of what had attempted to run her off of the road. She didn't even know what the car looked like. The color, make and model, approximate age, nothing. What help would that be?

"Well, I was...um, I was on my way home late last night—not too late, I was coming from my parents' new house. I was taking a backway to get to my place faster, but I realized someone was following me..."

Jonah had a feeling he knew where this story was going, but his facial expression didn't change as he continued to listen. Did something happened after she'd left the field office? His stomach knotted up with dread as he realized...

That was exactly what happened.

"...I turned onto a different road and was alone again for a few seconds, but then they followed me all the way down to the bridge that goes across Boulder River. They bumped me a few times, then tried to push my car down the hill and into the river—but I was able to outsmart them and save myself from going into the river just in time. They sped off after that."

Jonah took a deep breath in and rubbed his face with his hands, but he didn't want to be the first to speak. As much as he wanted to confront Rayne and demand why she didn't come to him after her near death, he knew to stay out of it until their boss gave her input and made the decision to include this incident in their investigation or not.

Bex placed her hands on her hips and started to pace around the small room, thinking. "Did you get any info?" she asked.

"Uh, no. I never got to confront the driver because they were already gone by the time I drove my car back up onto the street." Rayne said, disappointment in her voice.

"Did you see the car at all?"

"Not exactly, but I know that it was big, like an SUV or a pickup. With abnormal lights, almost yellow."

"This is insane." Leigh Crenshaw interjected, clearly becoming annoyed by the tone in her voice. "We don't need any false accounts that could potentially steer us off course with this investigation. We don't have anything that can prove that this actually happened!"

"This isn't a false account." Rayne tried to stay calm and respectful, but it was becoming harder by the minute. "This really happened. And I have a feeling this has something to do with my parents' attempted murder."

"Matter of fact, I'd like to have a discussion with you, if you don't mind; your mother's sister's story isn't adding up and now, neither is yours."

"You mean interrogate me?" Rayne scoffed.

"Why, yes, Agent Winters. Interrogate you." Leigh stated.

Rayne looked over at Bex for help, who had now stopped pacing, but to her surprise, none was given.

"I think you should go talk with Special Agent Crenshaw." Bex was siding with Leigh. "With what we've learned about Ms. Alistair, it can prove helpful for us."

Jonah was watching this all unfold, completely astounded. *There's no way they think she's making this up*, he thought angrily. *They're better agents than that.*

Leigh didn't wait for a response from Rayne as she walked past her and out the door, going in the direction of the interrogation rooms. Bex followed, letting the glass door close silently behind her.

There was an unbearable silence for a few moments. Then Jonah stood and spoke up. "Why didn't you tell me?"

"The same reason I was thinking about not telling anyone at all: there's no evidence. I have no idea who could've did this, but I know for sure it's related to our case."

"You could have at least came to me if not anyone else." he said. He walked up to her so that they were only mere inches apart. "I would have believed you—I believe you now. Please, I don't want you to keep things like this from me. This could have cost you your life."

"I'm sorry. Really, I am. I've just been having a hard time and I'm a bit overwhelmed."

"It's completely okay to feel that way, Rayne. But you have to open up to me and know that I'm here for you. I know you feel like you've betrayed me, but—"

"I did."

"You didn't betray me at all. Please know that we're in this together. You have to trust me."

"Why aren't you mad at me?"

"I can never be mad at you, Rayne."

She didn't say anything else after that.

"You'd better go deal with Leigh. Let me know how it goes."

• • •

Rayne awkwardly sat down in the cold steel chair that was bolted to the floor in the interrogation room. She silently watched as Leigh Crenshaw sat on the opposite side of her and crossed her arms.

Many moments passed where neither of them said a word to each other. The air in the room was thick with tension. Leigh didn't break her stance, staring menacingly as if trying to read her mind. Well, she is a criminal psychologist, Rayne thought. She's supposed to get inside people's heads.

"Did you make up this story?" Leigh asked simply.

Rayne blinked. "What? Of course not!" She tried to keep her voice monotone and stay cool and collected, but she couldn't help but to be utterly flabbergasted at Agent Crenshaw's question.

"You were just fine until Bex kicked you off of the case. Now all of a sudden you have an unknown assailant on your tail. Explain this to me again, please." Leigh retrieved a notepad and ballpoint pen.

Whatever psychology tactic she was using, Rayne was tired of it already. But she broke down her story for the second time, feeling worse than she had felt before.

"And you went directly home after that?"

"Yes."

"Why didn't you call 911 or go to the authorities? Why did you wait until this morning to come and tell us? In the middle of our meeting?"

"It was already late, and I knew the police wouldn't be able to do much anyway; I already checked the area and the driver was long gone. I doubt the neighborhood had any cameras on the street. And somehow my car left without a scrape on it."

"What's the name of the street?"

"It was Bellefonte Road."

Leigh thought for a moment. "Hm. I don't think that area has street surveillance, but it won't hurt to double check with the police department. But, why were you leaving at five a.m.? Why not wait until the sun came up to leave your parents' home?"

"I don't know. That was just the time I decided that I wanted to go home."

They sat in silence for a few more moments.

"Come on. You may be a rookie, but you're still a detective nonetheless. Even you know that your story is weak. No evidence, no known suspect, no lead. I'm going to have Anisa and Keon keep tabs on this while the rest of us deal with the task at hand."

"So, you're not going to make this a part of the main case?"

"Why should I? Would you, if the roles were reversed, Detective Winters?"

Rayne shook her head. "No. I suppose I wouldn't."

"I wanted to show you this." Leigh retrieved a piece of paper from a manila folder and slid it across the table. "What do you know about this?"

Rayne picked up the printed deal report and skimmed through it quizzically. "What...What is this?"

Leigh huffed. "Your aunt Ms. Simone and I had a discussion about her book deal. It's a memoir. But there's something else, and she's not saying what that is. Would you have any idea on what that could be? Or perhaps more insight on what this book will be about?"

Rayne was at a loss for words as she let the paper fall back down onto the table. She shook her head. "No. I don't know anything about this at all. I know she's a public speaker and a life coach and gets to travel and do all of these cool things and she gets invited to all these places, but I didn't know she wrote a memoir. When was this released?"

"The deal was made public not too long ago, at least that's what Simone said. But, she said the book is based on her life—and your mother's. Is there anything significant that you can think of that'd happened in their lives that could potentially go in a book? Like a traumatic event?" Leigh said.

"I don't know much about my mother's childhood, or my aunt's. I don't know what this could be about other than what the book description says."

Leigh was about to prod more when the door to the interrogation room swung open with a small creak, revealing Agent Anisa Ray.

"Chief wants you to see this," Ray said, speaking only to Leigh. "Our security cameras were breached."

● ● ●

Jonah and Rayne stood quietly outside of the security room while techs Anisa Ray and Keon Toussaint briefed Bex and Special Agent Leigh Crenshaw on their unusual discovery.

"What did they find?" Rayne said in a low voice, not wanting anyone—especially Leigh—to hear her.

Jonah stood with his arms crossed, leaning against the wall. "I think Keon said someone cut off the security cameras between three and five a.m. The whole grid went dark, then went back online as if nothing happened. They're trying to determine if it was an internal error or something outside that was tampering with it."

Rayne gasped. "Wait. That's around the same time my notes went missing." she whispered. "Do you think..."

Their gazes locked. They were both thinking the same thing.

"Someone must've came here, cut the feed, and stole them." Jonah concluded. "It could have very well been the suspect that we're after. How they had the ability to access our servers, I don't know, but whoever did this clearly has skill and resources. That could help us ID our suspect and catch them quicker."

"I can't tell anyone that my notes are missing." Rayne said. "I wasn't even supposed to be here looking for them in the first place. No one can know."

Jonah nodded solemnly. "I understand, but this could be a crucial piece of information for us—"

"No. Leigh is already skeptical of the story I told her. If I add that I was here alone looking for notes from a case that I'm not even supposed to be on anymore, that'll only make things worse and make me look guilty. That can't happen."

Jonah sighed. "Alright. I won't tell anyone. But I'm still going to look into this myself. If I find anything else out, I'll let you know asap."

"That means a lot to me, it really does. I just don't want you to get into trouble. But the sooner we catch who did this, the better."

• • •

The figure watched as rookie Detective Rayne Winters exited the Ruxlor City FBI Field Office in a hurry. She walked in strides down to the rear parking lot behind the building, hugging herself in her small peacoat to brace against the bitter autumn winds. She got into her car that was parked away from the rest of the vehicles, slamming the door with extra anger as she sat down, and remained there for about fifteen minutes as it warmed up to a more bearable temperature. The figure could tell that she was tired, and becoming utterly helpless.

To their content, the old silver BMW didn't wear any noticeable scrapes or scratches that displayed evidence of what had went down early that morning. Good. They'd failed to complete the job the first time, and they didn't need any more minor inconveniences that could blow their cover. They watched as Rayne put her car into Drive and sped away from the building, seemingly in a hurry to leave.

They wouldn't fail this time, though. They were counting on it.

14

JONAH PARKED THE BLAND, AGENCY-ISSUED sedan that was mostly used for undercover assignments on the side of Bellefonte Road and got out, surveying the area as he closed the door. He wore jeans, a black jacket, and basic sunglasses to conceal most of his face, looking inconspicuous, as he'd intended. He saw the aging bridge a few dozen yards ahead, the brown river that ran below it, and the steep embankment structure that Rayne had described to him earlier. It was mostly made of boulders and netting; if her car would have indeed been pushed off of the road, it would have slid all the way down into the river with no hopes of stopping.

He walked forward, soon seeing the black tire streaks where Rayne had slammed on her breaks to save herself—just about a foot away from being launched off of the cliffside. He snapped a quick photo with his work phone, then continued on. He walked down most of the barren residential street before turning around and heading back to the car. To his disappointment, there were no security cameras on any of the poles or cell towers, at least to his knowledge. He went from house to house, asking residents if they'd seen or heard any commotion around the time the incident occurred, but no one was saying anything.

Discouraged, Jonah got back in the car and made the short trip down the block to the police station.

"My partner and I did pull over someone who was driving a bit recklessly," an officer was saying, "I want to say at around five-fifteen a.m., but we let him off with a warning."

"Just a warning?" *Rayne's right. He's probably long gone by now*, Jonah thought sourly. But he couldn't give up hope.

The officer nodded slowly. "Yes, a warning. He was only going ten over the speed limit but he did blow a stop sign a little way's past the bridge."

"Okay. Well, can you say what the vehicle looked like? Make and model? Was it big?"

The officer shrugged. "Just your average heavy-duty pickup. Looked like it had a few mods on it. Nothing fancy."

Jonah thanked him for his time and left the station then, driving in the direction of the field office.

• • •

The dazzling upper south side of Ruxlor City was even more stunning with its fall ambience as Simone Alistair drove past the chic and trendy eateries, boutiques, shops, and dog parks. She usually came here for retail therapy, frequenting this part of town often, but today she was looking for someone important. Someone she needed to talk to urgently. She glumly passed all of her favorite stores and entered a quiet neighborhood of modernized duplexes and rowhouses, coming to a stop in front of the largest one and cutting off her engine. She brought down her mirror to adjust her blood-red lipstick and put on her cat-eye sunglasses before stepping out of the car and walking up the seemingly never ending staircase to reach the house. Today, she wore an outfit similar to what she wore at the FBI headquarters: a form-fitting black designer dress with heeled boots that went up to her knees, stockings, and plenty of gold jewelry on both of her wrists and neck.

When she made it to the front door, she knocked. When there was no answer, she knocked again, harder and louder this time. Finally she heard the footsteps of an approaching figure on the other side. One of the glass double doors slowly opened, just wide enough for a man's head to peek out.

"Simone? What are you doing here? I told you not to be coming around here." the man said in a low tone.

"I don't care about all that; we need to talk." Simone said. "Let me in, we can't talk outside."

The man huffed, obliging as he opened the door wider so Simone could step through into the foyer of his modernly designed residence. He was around her age, dressed in slacks and an expensive collared shirt, holding a glass of whiskey in one hand. A flashy diamond watched sparkled on his wrist. "Have you been watching the news?" he asked as he watched Simone help herself to her own glass at the bartop in the kitchen.

"Who watches news anymore?" she waved her hand in dismissal.

"You do know Evan is dead, right?"

Simone nodded.

"And the lady who was writing that article? Patrice?"

She nodded again.

"The local media is starting to quiet down when it comes to talking about their murders, but they were in fact using the word 'murder,' so now you know the city is speculating. And they're still stirring the pot when it comes to finding him."

"Him?"

"Yes. Him."

"They'll never find him."

The man scoffed. "And how do you know that for sure?" He downed the last of his whiskey.

"The media doesn't even know who they're talking about yet, his identity is still a mystery. At least to the public, anyway. The police aren't giving them much to go off of, and the FBI never released a statement to the news regarding their plans, so they're just saying anything at this point to keep people fearful." Simone stepped up to him now. "And why are you so uneasy all of a sudden? You're not thinking of backing out now, are you?"

The man she was speaking to was Tony Labrecque: the A-list executive producer of a documentary that was going to make Simone's career take off to new heights.

If they survived long enough to see the end of production.

"One of our producers is dead." Tony reminded her.

"Yes." Simone said. "One of them."

"And so is a journalist who was about to revisit the original cases."

"Perhaps she was working on another story that she was digging too deep into that got her killed. This project was never even made public yet; Evan and Patrice's deaths couldn't possibly be related to this."

"Then what about your sister?"

Simone stopped short, not knowing what to say.

"She's the real star of the show here." Tony went on. "Without her, this production would be nothing. She was targeted in an attempt to be silenced permanently. Someone doesn't want this story out, and they'll do just about anything to keep it in the dark—even commit murder."

"I don't care about who may or may not want this story to be told, Tony. This isn't just Neevah's story, this is my story too! I also suffered at the hands of this madman, and I won't let him win."

"If Neevah was dead, would you be saying the same thing?"

She paused. "The show must go on. If you won't do it, I'll find someone else who will." Simone put the glass on the countertop with unnecessary force before turning and storming out the door. Tony watched her leave, then swore under his breath as he poured himself another glass.

• • •

Smithson East Hospital was full and bustling as usual when Rayne stepped into the main building that evening. She took the route that she'd now memorized by heart to the state-of-the-art burn recovery unit, checked in, and waited for her parents' nurses to give her a report.

"They are both showing remarkable progress." a nurse was saying as she and Rayne walked down the corridor to the room. "For Owen, his pain has greatly subsided and he's no longer heavily dependent on pain medicines to keep him comfortable. We change his bandages throughout the day to make sure there's no infection. His mobility is still limited, but he's determined to make a speedy recovery."

"And what about my mother?" Rayne asked as they were approaching the door.

"As for Neevah, she's back in stable condition, which we are all happy about. She's not awake yet, but we are anticipating that to happen very soon."

They stepped into the room, and Rayne sat down in a vacant chair beside her father as the nurse began to chart vitals on a mobile computer stand. She gripped her father's hand, and he stirred.

"Rayne?" he said in a raspy voice that was barely above a whisper.

"Yes, Dad. It's me." Rayne moved her chair closer to the bed. "How're you feeling?"

Owen's face seemed to have aged overnight. He looked battered and tired, and he was still very well fighting for his life. He breathed in deeply. "Did...did they catch him?"

"Catch who, Dad? Who's him?"

"Did they...?"

"We didn't make any arrests yet, Dad. I'm so sorry. But you don't have to worry, we're doing everything we can to find who was responsible for this. I've actually been doing some—"

Owen's eyes opened wider, and he strained his head to look over at his daughter. "You...need to get off that case...immediately."

"Bex already kicked me off of the investigation, and now you're telling me to drop it too? I need to find out who did this to you. We can't give up..."

"No...my dear. You don't understand. It's not...safe here. You're not safe."

"What are you talking about?"

"None of us...will be safe. Not until...he's caught." He coughed lightly. "You have to go, Rayne....Do you understand? Leave town for a while. You can't...be caught up in all of this."

Rayne shook her head. "I don't understand. You know the man that targeted you and Mom?"

A monitor beside Owen started to beep repetitively, and a nurse walked in and reset it. "Miss Winters, I think Owen needs to rest now." she said. By now, Owen's eyes were closed again. He had drifted back off to sleep, snoring lightly. "Talking requires a lot of energy right now." the nurse explained as Rayne stood. "Energy that he doesn't currently have. He must've worn himself out. He also had a long physical therapy session this morning that's contributing to his tiredness. I'm sure he'll be up by tomorrow."

Dejected, Rayne left the hospital. She wanted to wake up her father and ask him more questions, but she also wanted him to rest. *I can always come back later and talk to him some more*, she thought as she waited for the valet driver to bring around her car. During the silent and uneasy drive home, umpteen questions were swarming around in her head, and her mind replayed the words that Owen had said.

Did they catch him?

It's not safe here.

You're not safe.

Leave.

Her father knew information that she didn't.

Information that could very well change the entire course of the investigation.

Not knowing who else to turn to, she dialed Jonah's number.

He answered on the first ring. "Detective Davenport."

"Hey, it's me. I have some updates that you definitely need to hear. This'll change everything about the case."

"Wait, what? You do? How?"

"We shouldn't discuss this over the phone, though. Are you still at headquarters?"

"I left a while ago. I'll just come to your place and we can talk there. But...Are you sure this will change everything?"

Rayne paused for just a moment. Then she said, "I'm absolutely sure."

• • •

At Rayne's apartment later that night, Jonah sat opposite of her at the small dining room table, sifting through his own notes. His laptop lay open in his lap. "I can't believe it." he said. "You're telling me Owen knows who targeted him and Neevah?"

"And potentially Brentwood and Latimore." Rayne said. She had relayed her entire conversation with her father back to Jonah, who sat perplexed.

"If your father thinks you're a target, then he's right; you should get out of the city for a while." Jonah added. "At least until we make an arrest."

"That's not happening." Rayne said simply. "I'm not going to rest until I find this person. Nothing is going to make me back down." She paused as she scrolled through articles on her own laptop.

"Does anything Owen said correlate with what Leigh told you during your interrogation?" Jonah asked.

"I do remember Leigh telling me that my aunt confessed to someone trying to hurt my mom, like a stalker or something. But she didn't say much else. Maybe the persona the 'Humble Creek Killer' that's on the title of the book. Also, my dad referred to them as a 'he,' so I think it's safe to say we can now assume our suspect is a male, but still be open to them being a woman as well. Wait, I think I found something..." Her voice trailed off as an article caught her attention, and she clicked on it to open it. "This is it." She took a few minutes to fully read over the old newspaper article that had been scanned and uploaded to a news site, then handed over her laptop to Jonah so he could see.

"You think this is the guy we need to be hunting down?" he said.

"I'm one hundred percent positive."

"But, how were Evan Brentwod and Patrice Latimore involved with this guy? And why's this guy wreaking havoc now, all this time later?"

"I don't know, but I'm sure the rest of our questions will be answered in due time. That's our suspect, I know it." Rayne pointed at the computer Jonah was holding. "We find him, and we find answers."

Jonah also had Simone's book deal pulled up on his laptop to compare to the article Rayne had discovered. It was pretty vague, but it did have *Surviving the Humble Creek Killer* as the subtitle.

The newspaper article was similarly titled. A FAMILY IN FEAR: HUMBLE CREEK STALKER ATTACKS AFTER ESCAPING CUSTODY. Rayne's mother, aunt, and grandparents were pictured on the first page, looking like they were walking out of a building of some kind. It explained that this particular stalker was common to the townspeople of Humble Creek and had been terrorizing randomly selected people for a few years, which was, to Jonah's and Rayne's surprise, only thirty minutes outside of the city. This criminal used the same tactics as the suspect they were hunting now: arson. Rayne's mother was caught in the crosshairs, and allegedly, she was close to catching him, but he got away by the time police had arrived.

Could this new reign of terror be from a copycat killer, or the original culprit? Jonah wondered. Both were plausible, but they didn't have strong evidence to prove the copycat scenario. They had to have been dealing with the same guy. "I can't believe this happened to your mother." he said, still in a state of disbelief. "Your aunt said he almost killed her. Maybe she was close to catching him once and for all, but he managed to vanish after a violent confrontation."

"That's what I'm thinking." Rayne said. "The title suggests that this guy was in custody before. Maybe if we do some digging and find his identity, that'll bring us one step closer to locating him. I'll also talk to my dad again sometime tomorrow when he's rested up. We need to know more before we present this to Bex; I want this to be solid. If it's not, I may lose my job for not listening and staying out of this."

Jonah nodded. "Agreed. But, we have to do this together. With a potential target on your back, there's no way you should be doing this by yourself. I'll keep quiet at the office so Bex and Leigh don't grow suspicious. Promise me you won't pursue any new leads alone."

"Jo, I—"

"Promise me, Rayne." he said more intently. "That's all I'm asking."

She sighed. "Alright. I promise. I appreciate you wanting to help me—"

Just then, Jonah's work phone buzzed in his back pocket. "Sorry, I have to take this." He retrieved it and answered the call.

When he hung up, he didn't say anything.

15

HUES OF RED AND BLUE STILL basked the scene of the crime when Jonah arrived and parked his Jeep on the sidewalk. He noticed he was somewhere on the outskirts of town, the skyscrapers sparkling in the distance in an azure-blue sky. Police cruisers and two firetrucks blocked off both sides of a rundown road that seemed to have been abandoned and neglected long ago. He got out of his truck, flashed his badge, and was granted access to the street. He began a slow, apprehensive walk closer to the commotion.

"It was a false alarm." Bex called out when she'd noticed Jonah had arrived to do an investigation and get intel. She walked towards him, wearing white gloves and a black FBI cap along with her typical attire.

Jonah's eyes narrowed as they halted in front of each other. "False alarm?"

"There's no body here."

"Says who?"

"Says the chief medical examiner of the city, that's who."

Jonah peered past her over to the alleged crime scene. There was yellow caution tape blocking off what seemed to be an old commercial building, but there wasn't much else. Nothing to mark evidence with, no forensics crew. In fact, it looked like everyone was packing up, preparing to leave.

Bex looked at him quizzically. "It was an arsonist's work down here. Didn't find any fingerprints. Do you still want to check it out?" Jonah nodded once. She waved over an officer in uniform. When they got closer, Jonah saw by the style of the uniform that he was the chief of police for Ruxlor City. "I'm gonna let Detective Davenport do one more sweep of the perimeter." Bex told the sheriff. "Then we'll wrap this up."

"Will do, Chapman." the police chief said. "If you need anything, you know where to find us." They shook hands briefly, and the officer headed back down to the opposite side of the street where his car was parked.

"The fire took a while to contain, but it was put out about ten minutes ago." Bex explained. "The firemen said it most likely started in what used to be the basement of that building right there." She pointed to a crumbling red brick building that was about five storeys tall, all of the windows busted, vines growing around the sides. "Then it worked its way upward, as you can see with all the smoke still in the air above the open roof."

"And you're sure nothing was found in the basement?" Jonah asked.

"Certain of it. But I'm granting you permission to look again. Make it quick, though. We don't need to hold up the police department or the firemen."

"Where's the rest of the squad?"

"I sent them all home. I told them the same thing I'm telling you: it was a false alarm, and there's no further purpose for the FBI to be here. The firefighters are taking over from here."

Jonah already knew what he was going to do, but he pretended to ponder anyway. He gave a dramatic sigh. "Actually...that's okay, Chief. If no one's seen anything by now, then there's no body here. We can go now."

He would come back later, when the commotion had died down, so he could conduct his own investigation, alone.

"I'll have agents keep tabs on this place for the time being, but it looks as though it was a regular fire; the report that I was given said that building was already abandoned after a foreclosure two decades ago, and no one's inhabited it since. It was already empty when the fire began." Bex glanced at her watch, which read seven-thirty p.m. Then the sound of tires rolling on gravel caught her attention. She squinted beyond them to the beginning of the road. "Looks like news vans coming in. I suggest we leave now before they spot us. The public is already starting to buzz, we don't want to give them anything more to talk about."

Jonah agreed, not wanting to get caught in the crosshairs of the vexing local media. He hurried to climb into his Jeep and sped away.

• • •

It was a few degrees cooler when he returned, the road now pitch black omit his high beams. Jonah parked in the exact same spot he had before on top of the sidewalk, killed the engine, and stepped out of his car. He slipped on a pair of white gloves and held a small flashlight in one hand. He was no longer wearing his usual professional work attire, now dressed in mainly black; black shoes, jeans, leather jacket, to help blend into the darkness and avoid being spotted by anyone who could be roaming around this part of town.

He slowly crept up to the building in an armed stance, the smell of smoke still lingering in the air, and ducked under the caution tape that was still surrounding the perimeter. He carefully stepped over piles of rubble and rocks and entered the old structure.

The place was beyond uninhabitable and difficult to maneuver around, but that didn't mean a crime could not have been committed here. To Jonah's dismay, it could very well be the opposite—the emptiness of the area with no people around it, the discreet location, the darkness. It was the perfect spot for the perfect crime...He found an opening that led to what seemed to be the basement level, and he descended down, rocks and debris crushing beneath his feet. The air was stale down here, permeated by dust and potentially mold, and he couldn't help but begin to cough. He moved his flashlight around to reveal that he was in a relatively small space; he was expecting a massive room.

There's nothing down here, he thought to himself, dispirited. *They were right*. He turned to head back up the weathered stairs.

But just then, he heard sounds above him—footsteps on top of crumbling rock.

Someone else was here.

Jonah withdrew his .30 handgun in one swift motion and dashed up the stairs. He approached a dark figure whose identity was unknown. He shined his flashlight on their face while trying to keep his gun steady in his other hand, but the figure recoiled at the blinding light and darted in the other direction.

"Hey! FBI—freeze!" Jonah sprinted after them.

A bullet fired back at him in response, just barely grazing his left shoulder and hitting the wall behind him. It stung his skin, causing him to grunt and stop in his tracks. But he couldn't lose his new opponent, whoever they were, they were fast and putting more distance between them by the second. He dropped his flashlight to grip his shoulder and apply pressure to the scrape and kept his gun held firmly in his right hand. He picked up speed again, running outside to see the figure already almost halfway down the street. Jonah didn't want to use his gun, it was more of a safety measure for himself, and there was no other way to stop his opponent from this far away. He squinted into the darkness of the night to try to see who had targeted him, but it was no use.

They got away.

•••

It was a cold and bitter Monday morning when Rayne visited the hospital to see her parents. More specifically, she was going to speak to her father Owen, hoping to finish the conversation that was started the last time she was here.

Did they catch him?

It's not safe here.

You're not safe.

Leave.

She needed answers. And if for some reason Owen wasn't going to give them to her, then she would find them another way.

By traveling to Humble Creek herself.

The newspaper articles that she and Jonah had read in her apartment made her perceive the borough as a flourishing and vibrant small town where seemingly nothing could go wrong, but the reality was far from that. According to her aunt's book in progress, wave of terror had reigned there, causing the trajectory of Simone's and her mother's lives to change forever. And clearly, that terror had returned.

But why?

Rayne parked her BMW at the valet drop off and got out of her car. She eagerly walked inside the hospital and made her way up to the room her mother and father were still staying in. She walked in the door to see Owen slowly but surely eating breakfast. A nurse spoon-fed him what looked to be oatmeal, then helped him sip orange juice from a straw. The burns were starting to heal on his face, but it still made it difficult to eat. She glanced over at the now barren space in the shared room where here mother once was. The nurses had moved Neevah to the room next door after they'd grown wary of Owen's mental state. He claimed he was fine, but the night-shift nurses informed Rayne that he had been having one-sided conversations with her at random times of the night, and, when she wouldn't answer, he'd burst into tears. They said it would be best for Owen to have some time to himself for awhile.

"Hey, Dad. How're you feeling?" Rayne asked when the nurse was done and began packing up the breakfast cart.

"Fine." Owen Winters said limply. He was now sitting up in his bed, his bandaged arms stretched out in front of him, his eyes not meeting hers. He'd remembered the last words he said the last time his daughter had come to see him.

"You need to tell me who we need to be tracking down." Rayne said when the nurse was out of earshot. She pulled up a vacant chair and sat beside the bed. "You asked me if they caught him, but who is he? Does he have a name? How do you know him?"

Owen drew in a shuddery breath. "I...can't tell you, Rayne."

"Why?"

"He'll come for you, too. I can't have that. If something were to happen to you, I'd never forgive myself. And your mother wouldn't either." He peered over at the connected room in which Neevah laid, still sleeping.

"We need to know who we're dealing with. It'll save the FBI a lot of time, and it'll put all of us out of harm's way."

"You don't understand..."

"Then help me understand." She gripped her father's hand at the bedside. "This is my job now. I'm a profiler. I'm close to cracking this, I can feel it. I just need a bit more evidence. And I'm not stopping until I find the criminal that did this."

Owen squeezed his eyes shut. "We should have never brought this back to light..."

"What do you mean?"

He shook his head, a single tear shedding from his eye. "I just want to protect you. But I can't in this condition. I'm useless."

"Don't say that, Dad. It's okay. I'm perfectly fine, I can take care of myself. Everything is going to be okay. You have to believe that."

When she was long gone, he pressed the Call button on the remote control at his bedside. His nurse came in, and he instructed her to hand him his cell phone since he couldn't bend his arms or legs just yet. He then called someone who he knew he could always rely on.

16

RAYNE HAD ALWAYS LOVED VISITING THE library as a child, and especially as she grew older, in middle school, high school, college, and even during her time in the FBI academy. To her, it was a haven, and held an infinite amount of knowledge. She eagerly parked her car on the sidewalk, placed a few quarters in the parking meter, and walked into the Ruxlor City Public Library, a tall sandstone building that sat right in the middle of Main Street in the heart of town. She'd memorized the floorplan by heart from years of frequenting here with her parents and old classmates, and went straight to the elevator at the back of the first floor, then descended down to the lower level where the county's print and digital archives were stored.

She walked up and down the numerous rows of massive ten-foot tall bookshelves in the dim room, searching. She knew exactly what she was looking for, but she wasn't hopeful that this library would have them. But, she had to try every possible avenue to acquire as much information as possible.

With no luck at the physical archives, she sat down at a vacant computer and conducted a simple search: *Humble Creek*.

Nothing.

She sucked in a breath and let it out slowly. If this simple search term didn't pull back any results, then she wasn't sure what would. Rayne left the library, but she was not deterred from finding more information about the Humble Creek Killer.

• • •

A dark gray overcast loomed in the sky as Jonah pulled into the visitor parking lot. A bitter wind enveloped him as he stepped out of his car and tightened his windbreaker jacket around his neck. A storm was coming, but he'd checked his cell phone and learned that he still had a good couple of hours to prepare, but he didn't need to do anything on his end. Whatever he already had inside his apartment would have to suffice if the storm got crazy. He went into the building and navigated to where he was instructed to go.

Arriving at the destination, he knocked on the door that was already ajar before stepping inside. The room was dim from the rapidly decreasing sunlight, but he could see the man laying in the bed, awaiting his arrival.

"Jonah?"

"I'm here, Mr. Winters."

Jonah sat down in a vacant chair that was at Owen Winters's bedside and placed a gentle hand on his shoulder. "How you holding up?"

"Physically, I am doing a lot better. But mentally...I'm weak."

"I'm here for you, Mr. Winters—we all are. The city, the squad..."

"Please, son, call me Owen, remember?"

Son. He hadn't called him that in so long. A pang of guilt tugged at his heart, and he let out a heavy sigh. "You called me saying you needed something from me?"

Owen glared warily at the door, as if someone was lurking on the other side of it. "I need you to find him before Rayne does, and take him down. Shoot to kill, if necessary."

Jonah shook his head. "But, Rayne's not on the assignment anymore. The director of our unit relieved her."

"That's not going to stop her from looking for him."

Owen could almost chuckle. "We both know how headstrong my daughter is. Once she commits to doing something, it's almost impossible to get her to change her mind. She told me herself; she's doing this with or without the FBI."

That wasn't what Jonah had expected to hear, but he vowed to Owen that he would keep his word. "We'll find him. The squad and I already have some new leads." But he could tell his words weren't making him feel any better. "We're getting close, I know it. You trust us, right?"

"I still have faith in the FBI, but the system has failed many times before, and I'm afraid it may fail again."

17

"WE HAVE A MOTIVE." BEX CHAPMAN stated cheerfully as Jonah walked into the conference room the following morning.

"We do?" Jonah questioned, raising an eyebrow as he sat down and opened his notes.

"Indeed." Bex waited for the rest of her agents to file into the room before continuing. "Our suspect has only targeted city residents who are highly influential, successful, well-known, or all of the above. If we can warn—"

"—But, Chief, if I could interject?" Jonah said, and Bex reluctantly nodded her approval. "That just doesn't seem right. I firmly believe Rayne is a target as well, and she doesn't match the descriptions of any of the victims before her. Her missing notes, for example, and the incident with the driver who tried to run her off the road in this very neighborhood.

Is this the reasoning we've come up with including her story?"

"No, that is our conclusion not taking Rayne's stories into account." Leigh said, who sat on the opposite end of the table. "And we're sticking to it. It's all we've got to go off of right now."

"I actually have some new findings that will change the entire direction of our investigation, and that will lead us straight to our perpetrator." Jonah spread out his laminated printouts of newspaper articles, website pages, and witness accounts that he and Rayne had found together. It mainly pertain to the soon-to-be-famous Humble Creek Killer thanks to Simone Alistair's book deal, and Rayne's mother's side of the family.

"So, we're going to be turning this whole investigation onto Rayne's family now?" Leigh said. "What about the other victims who have suffered? And their families?"

"Look. We're dealing with an arsonist, right?" Jonah said. Everyone nodded subtly. "Well, the Alistairs have experienced terror like this before, exactly how we're witnessing it now. All we need to do is figure out how all of the victims are connected, and it could lead us right to the culprit."

"But what if it's a copycat?" Senior Detective Diana Reeves asked as she skimmed over the articles. "All of this happened in the late eighties. While it is very plausible that this is the same killer we're hunting, we want to keep every possible scenario in mind, and leave no stone unturned. I've experienced both situations in my line of duty, but even I have to admit sometimes we didn't always put the right person behind bars."

"So what are you saying?" Jonah said.

"What I'm saying is, we shouldn't make this entirely about the Alistair family. This is solid research, yes, but I just don't think this is the right call to make. Not when there's other victims involved that have no relation to them at all."

"That's why it needs to be our next task to find how they're all connected."

"I think I'm going to end this here." Bex said, raising a hand to signal for the two agents to stop. "I highly appreciate your findings, Davenport. If you could, I'd like copies of those on my desk so I can take a further look. But our motive still stands. Today we're going to be revisiting everyone we'd interviewed. Not here at our headquarters, though. They'll be surprise visits. Davenport, I'm sending you with Agent Blackridge to Simone Alistair's residence. Reeves and Hall will go back to Valencia to scope out Patrice Latimore's home, and Crenshaw and I will go to Ms. Abbott's. See if their alibis are still the exact same. If any details have changed, even the smallest detail, or they seem to be hiding something,

I have search warrants on hand to see what they're hiding. Report everything back to me in an hour. Everyone got that?"

Everyone nodded.

"Good." Bex grinned. "Let's get to work."

...

Agent Sawyer Blackridge happily accompanied his rookie colleague as he drove an unmarked sedan to the posh and secluded Cliffmont Estates. When they reached the entrance to the community, it was gated, and they didn't have a keycard to pass through. Sawyer drove up to the kiosk and pressed the single button. A speaker was above it, and a grumpy sounding voice replied. "Who is it?"

"Agent Sawyer Blackridge, FBI."

A small sigh came from the speaker. Then the voice spoke again, "Hold on, I'm coming right out." A short and stocky security guard emerged from a nearby structure that they'd guessed was where security footage was kept, a grandiose recreational center behind it, equipped with a swimming pool, tennis court, playground, amphitheater, and dog park. The guard carefully but quickly made his way down the small hill to the gates where his eyes scanned over the vehicle and its two occupants, both dressed in black suits.

The older man, probably in his early to mid-fifties, if Jonah had to guess, was nearly huffing and puffing by the time he reached the driver's side window. The guard jutted out his chin, squinting at Sawyer. "You said you were FBI?"

"That's right. We're from the Ruxlor City field office." Sawyer showed his badge. "We need to get past and speak to a Miss Simone Alistair. She lives around here, right?"

"Yes, she does. I'll give her a call to see if she's expecting company." The guard almost turned around to head back to the building where he came from, but Sawyer cleared his throat and retrieved a piece of paper from inside his suit jacket's pocket.

"There's no need. This is a surprise visit." Sawyer handed him the neatly folded search warrant, and the security guard opened it to read it. Without saying anything else, the man turned and used his own keycard to unlock the iron gates, and they slowly creaked open. Sawyer thanked him, and the two of them continued on up the hill and into the housing community.

"They have cameras around the facilities." Jonah said. "We could check them later to match Simone's alibi."

"That'll help us down the road." Sawyer noted just as the GPS told them they were approaching the house. 977 Blossom Court was a grand Acadian-style, sandstone brick estate with a fountain in the middle of a roundabout-style driveway, rolling plains behind it, and three garages that were open to reveal two SUVs and one convertible. The silver Lexus truck, Jonah remembered, was sitting in the parking lot when Simone was first being interrogated. A well dressed middle-aged man was tending to the dying landscape that surrounded the stone water fountain, and he watched them park and get out of the car.

"Good afternoon, sir." Sawyer spoke first, walking up to him slowly. "I'm Agent Blackridge with the FBI. You're Miguel Ruiz?"

"Yes." the man said nervously, putting down his tools. "Can I help you with something?"

"We're looking for Simone. Is she here?"

"Yes, I can go get her." Miguel hurried into the house through two glass French doors. A few minutes later, Simone stepped out, fashionably dressed as usual, a cocktail of some sorts gripped in one hand.

"Who's here?" they heard her say as she was approaching. She squinted when she recognized the agents' faces. "What are you two doing here at this hour?"

"We're just asking everyone a few more questions." Sawyer explained simply. "Won't take long."

Simone huffed loudly. "I already said everything I know. Why must I keep repeating myself?"

"We understand your frustration, Ms. Alistair, but this is just part of our general process and can be proven very helpful when making crucial decisions, especially with major cases such as this. Now, do you mind if we come inside and chat?"

"I do mind, actually." Simone took a sip from her glass.

"So, you won't talk to us again?" Jonah asked.

"No."

"That's fine, Miss Alistair," Sawyer waved the search warrant with one hand, "we have everything we need right here." He brushed past her and started towards the house.

"B-But," Simone stammered, stunned. "Why is there a search warrant for my house? I certainly don't have anything to hide."

Miguel Ruiz remained standing where he was a few feet away, speechless. Jonah gave him an apologetic look before following behind his superior. Sawyer started in the large foyer, opening a single drawer beside the front doors that kept old mail and miscellaneous items, then closed the drawer and entered the garage through a closed door. When it was determined that there was nothing of interest inside the garage, Jonah followed Sawyer as he walked around to the side of the house where he'd discovered a small tool shed, and opened it. He put on white gloves, handing a pair to Jonah as well, and retrieved a flashlight from his suit pocket.

"What are we looking for, exactly?" Jonah asked. "Things that were also found on our other crime scenes?"

"Exactly." Sawyer nodded. "It can be something so simple that can be easily overlooked, so keep your eyes peeled. You remember what we found at our victims' homes that we believe was used to start the fires?"

"Methanol and kerosene. One or both can birth the perfect explosion."

"Bingo." Sawyer continued to rummage around the tool shed. He came across a red gasoline canister that was about half full, most likely for a lawn mower or the home's massive power generator that they'd passed walking over to the shed, but he moved it over just an inch to see something was behind it, almost as if it was hiding. With his gloved hand, he picked up the tiny translucent blue bottle and examined it under the bright light of his flashlight. It didn't have a cap on it. He lifted it to his nose and took a sniff. "Smell that." he passed it to Jonah.

Jonah cautiously sniffed the bottle and recoiled. "Ugh. Smells like alcohol."

"That's what methanol smells like."

The same highly flammable liquid that was found in Evan Brentwood's living room where he had burned to death. Small traces of it had also been found in Patrice Latimore's home, and in the most recent fire that had happened on the outside of the city.

"I'll handle Simone. You call the forensics crew here ASAP to try to run some fingerprints and DNA off of that bottle."

Jonah nodded and placed the bottle right where they'd found it, behind the can of gasoline. He followed his fellow agent out of the shed and pulled out his work phone, dialing the number to the Violent Crimes' office. As he put the phone up to his ear and waited for someone to pick up, he watched as Sawyer confronted Simone a few feet away.

"Simone Alistair, you're under arrest for the murder of Evan Brentwood."

Simone stammered as she was put into the cold silver handcuffs and was recited her rights. "What?! B-But, I don't even know the guy. You've made a huge mistake! Honey! Call our lawyer!"

Miguel Ruiz scrambled to retrieve his cell phone from his back pocket and attempted to get ahold of their lawyer as he watched his fiancée getting placed in the back of the sedan. "Wait!" he said breathlessly before the agents made their exit. "Where are you taking my fiancée?"

"She'll be in the city jail." Sawyer said flatly and hopped in the driver's seat, closing the door. Simone yelped when she heard where she would be going and began to wail. Jonah sat in the passenger seat, and they drove off, en route to the Ruxlor City Jail.

18

"**DON'T TELL RAYNE THAT I'M MEETING** with you privately, okay, Mr. Winters?"

"Just call me Owen, son. You've always been like a son to me, you know that?" Owen Winters responded with a faltering smile, shifting in the black loveseat, trying to get comfortable with all of the bandages and gauze he had been taped up with. He was granted permission to leave his hospital room for lunch, retreating in a peaceful and scenic lounge outside of Smithson East's cafeteria. "And I won't tell her about you coming here. Is it important?"

"Yes. It's very important." Jonah said. "I need you to be completely honest with me, alright?"

"Of course, Jonah. What is it?"

Jonah lowered his voice so no one would overhear their conversation. "I'm going to tell you a few names, and you need to tell me if you know them or not."

Owen stopped eating. "Alright. I can do that."

"Okay...Evan Brentwood."

He pondered. "...Yes."

"Patrice Latimore?"

"Yes."

"You're telling me you know both of these people?" Jonah was baffled.

"Yes, vaguely. But I do not know them personally."

"And how exactly do you know them?"

"They..." Owen sighed and averted his gaze to the floor. "They are—well, I guess they were—part of the production group for the film deal Neevah's family got."

"A film deal?"

"Yes—but, it was never announced. We were still in the pre-production phase when the attacks started happening. The official announcement wasn't going to be made until December. It's nearing the end of October now."

"What is it supposed to be about?"

"The Humble Creek Arsonist." Owen said in just above a whisper. "He was a stalker and a serial murderer. But mainly the Alistairs and how they were the final family to overcome his reign of terror before he supposedly vanished. It was going to be called *Surviving Evil* or something like that. But...I wonder if they will still finish the production or not."

Jonah nodded, jotting everything down. "Is Neevah on the executive board for this?"

"No, but Simone is. She oversees a lot of it."

"I see. Thank you for your time, Owen. Take care of yourself, and stay alert and stay vigilant. I'll keep in touch."

Owen nodded silently and tried to smile, showing signs of tiredness. "I appreciate everything you and the department are doing for me and my family. You're a good kid. I hope you know that."

Now it was his turn to be silent. He mouthed his thanks as he gathered his things and left.

PART FOUR

19

IT WAS A FEW DAYS LATER, a bitter and damp weekend, and it had been raining nonstop. Ominous dark clouds loomed over the city, giving an eerie atmospheric feel to the residents of Ruxlor. It casted a darkness over the typical hustle and bustle in which most people didn't pay any attention to. Ruxlor City was naturally an innovative, up-and-coming but sometimes gritty place, but if one was here long enough, they'd learned how to live with it.

Danger was never too far from the townspeople.

Jonah sat alone at a small café that was buzzing with businesspeople, students, and those just looking for a change of scenery, pondering. Should he tell Rayne about the conversation he'd had with her father? He was sworn to secrecy, but this ultimately changed everything about their investigation. This was a family matter, which would be to

Bex's and Leigh Crenshaw's dismay. Did he even want to tell his superiors about the new information? He knew he had to. As a detective for the FBI, he couldn't simply withhold information just for the sake of doing so. He picked up his work phone from the table and dialed Bex Chapman's number.

"FBI Field Office, Violent Crimes Division. This is Chapman."

"Chief, it's me. I've got some new information." Jonah said in a low tone. Although he was sitting in a booth tucked away in the back of the café, no average civilian needed to hear what he was saying.

"That's good, Davenport. What did you find?"

"I went to speak with Owen Winters, and he knew both Patrice Latimore and Evan Brentwood. Not on a personal level, but they were all working together."

"Working together? On what? A—"

Suddenly, a sonorous boom erupted in the distance, and he knew it wasn't thunder. People didn't seem to care too much about the noise, assuming it was just the worsening rain. But when a bright red-orange glow broke through the storm, giving away the location of the disturbance, a few customers peered out of the tall windowpanes, pointing and staring. Worrisome whispers spread through the café like wildfire.

"Chief, did you hear that, by chance?"

"I did." Bex responded. "Sounded like an explosion. I'm trying to get a location on it now."

Jonah stood, abandoning his pastries and coffee. "It looks like it came from the south, just outside the city."

"You don't have to shadow this one if you don't want to. I'll have Agent Blackridge meet me there. You just make a record of you interviewing Mr. Winters, and we'll talk about what he said when this wraps up."

"Okay. I guess I can sit this one out." Jonah sat back down and took a sip of his coffee, but he still felt slightly on edge. Maybe it was just the caffeine getting into his system and messing with his nerves.

"Great. I'll call you back once we have a report." Bex hung up, the line going dead, and Jonah let out a dull sigh. He decided to call Rayne.

She answered on the first ring. "Did you hear that?" was the first thing she said.

"You heard it, too?"

"Yeah, and that orange glow...do you think it was a bomb?"

"I don't know. Bex is supposed to be calling me back when she finds out."

"Are you going to check it out?"

"No, I'm sitting this one out. Sawyer's going to meet Bex at the site."

"Oh, good...I kind of didn't want you going over there anyway."

"Why?"

"I don't know. I just don't have a good feeling about any of this. The more we dig into this, the worse I feel."

"Me neither, but we're much closer to solving this now. I know it."

"How are you so sure—?"

An incoming call buzzed in Jonah's ear. "That's probably Bex. I have to take this, but I'll call you back. Are you home?"

"Yeah, I am. I've been here for a while."

"Good. Stay there, and don't leave until we get this under control. Got it?"

"Okay. I'll stay."

"I'll call you back." Jonah hung up and pressed a button to pick up the new call. "Detective Davenport."

"Davenport, it's me again. It was a diversion. The entire place is empty. There's nothing here."

"Really? With that big of a commotion we just saw?"

"This guy is messing with us big time. I called in forensics to photograph everything and collect samples of the debris when the firefighters are done putting the flames out, but this definitely looks like an explosion of some kind."

"A diversion..." Jonah said more to himself than to his boss.

What could this be distracting them from?

"Wait," Jonah said. "What time is it?"

"Five till eleven."

Then he realized. *Eleven o'clock. Mr. Winters is getting discharged at eleven. As a living victim, he might have a target on his back again...*He swore under his breath. "I gotta go, Chief. We'll talk about what I uncovered later today." He hung up without waiting for Bex to respond and left the café in a hurry. He found his Jeep where he'd left it on the sidewalk, climbed in, and took off. He mouthed a silent prayer of relief as he cruised down Maxwell Run Highway going just above the speed limit. He was making good time. There was very little traffic going outbound, granted that it was a Saturday afternoon and weekday rush hour didn't typically start until two o'clock anyway, and he was able to make it to Canobie Commons at 11:24.

He was able to pass through the gates after stating he was from FBI, and he sped down the block in the direction of the townhome community. As he was approaching the Winters' residence, he witnessed a taxi slow to a stop in front of the house, and someone struggled to get out. It was Owen

Winters. Jonah parked haphazardly at the intersection and killed the engine. But just as he was getting out, he noticed someone else was walking down the avenue. A tall, dark figure in all black clothes, hood pulled tight over his head, he was speed-walking away from the Winters' house.

"Hey! Stop right there!" Jonah shouted.

Owen closed the door to the taxi and turned around, just now noticing his presence. He still wore his hospital bracelets and gray nonslip socks with his sliders and a brown jumpsuit, one hand still significantly bandaged up.

The figure continued to ignore Jonah and was now walking faster, almost in a jog. Now growing annoyed, Jonah made sure his .25 handgun was still in his holster just in case he needed to use it, and made sure his badge was securely fastened onto his shirt before starting down Swan Avenue. "Freeze! FBI!" After hearing those words, the figure broke into a sprint, turning onto another street and out of sight. Jonah took off after him, but the nameless man had quite a distance in front of him, and he didn't want to use his gun to slow him down and ultimately demobilize him. He cursed as he came to a stop to catch his breath, and he pulled his phone out of his pocket to call Bex, who, to his relief, immediately answered.

"Bex, I need backup at 1000 Swan Avenue, now. I've got a suspect running north of..." His voice trailed off as he walked back down the road to see Owen approaching the front door of his home. "Owen, no! Don't go in there!" He ran, quickly forgetting that he was on the phone, trying to reach the older man before something unhinged happened.

Jonah tackled him before he could begin to climb the stairs to the front door, just as a thunderous boom erupted from inside the house, glass from the windowpanes shattering into thousands of little pieces, raining onto them.

• • •

Rayne ducked under the caution tape that was hastily put up to deter residents from entering Swan Avenue and ran over to her father, who was now sitting in the back of an ambulance, being evaluated by an EMT. Owen Winters extended his arms and embraced his daughter with a tight squeeze. He winced from the pain of his burn wounds, but the instant relief of having his daughter by his side made him forget about the searing pain.

"I'm so glad you're okay, Dad." Rayne cried, burying her face into his shoulder.

"I'm alive and uninjured, thanks to Jonah."

Jonah had immediately called Rayne after securing backup from Bex, who then also sent the police down to try and track down the man Jonah had seen. "He saved you, right?" Rayne pulled back from their hug and looked at her dad's tired face.

Owen nodded, giving a small smile. "Such a good kid, always looking out for others and doing right by them. Sam and Serena raised him right."

Jonah was sitting in the back of a separate ambulance, next to the one Owen was in. Other than a scraped up elbow and hand, he was happily unscathed, and even happier knowing he had just saved Owen's life. He saw Rayne approaching and he cleared his throat, suddenly nervous. She wasn't dressed to brace the cold in just a t-shirt, leggings, and tennis shoes with her arms crossed over her chest; she'd no doubt run straight out of her condo and down the block without a second thought as soon as he had delivered the news to her. When she was less than a foot in front of him, he stood.

"Is it true?" she said, almost breathless from running. "You saved my father's life?"

Jonah nodded. Before he could open his mouth to speak, he felt her long arms wrap around his neck as she brought him into a tight embrace.

"Thank you." she whispered as tears stung her eyes.

He returned the embrace by wrapping his own arms around her small waist. "You don't need to thank me,

Rayne." He didn't dare let himself get emotional, not here, at least. "It's just part of the job."

She pulled back from the hug, but her hands still rested on his shoulders. "How'd you know my parents' new address?"

Jonah shrugged and broke their gaze, looking beyond her and at the agents coming in and out of the townhome, collecting evidence from the origin of the alleged bomb. "He didn't want me to tell you anything but...Owen wants me to help you. He doesn't want you doing this alone, especially since you don't have the FBI's protection on this one anymore. We had a discussion."

"About...?"

"He called me to the hospital a few days ago and I interviewed him there. He knows both of the victims by name—and so does Neevah. They were all working together on something, but I don't know what yet."

Rayne gasped and glanced at her father, who was still sitting in the back of the other ambulance. The EMT was assessing the bandages on his arms. "What do you think they could be doing together?"

Jonah sighed. "I don't know, but I have a feeling it has something to do with your aunt's book deal."

"Does the team know?"

"About Owen knowing the victims? Not yet. I only informed Bex about it when we both heard that explosion on the other end of town—what we think was just a diversion to distract us from this..." he nodded his head toward the house.

She shivered at the thought of her father almost falling victim to this ruthless killer—twice. Or maybe she was shivering out of fear, or from the bitter cold.

"I told my dad I was going to catch whoever did this to him and my mother, with or without the FBI. He tried to steer me away from this case, but this is my job—our job. I may have been taken off of the case on paper, but I'm not backing out of this. None of us are."

"You trust me to protect you, right?"

She looked at him. "It's not that I don't trust you, but...do you still trust me, after what I did?"

"You didn't do anything, Rayne."

"I did, though. I left you, right in the middle of everything you were going through. It's okay to acknowledge that I'm a horrible person for what I did. You didn't deserve that. And I don't deserve your help..."

"Don't think like that. None of what happened was your fault. You did what you needed to do at the time. There's nothing wrong with that."

"I know this sounds stupid, but..."

There was silence for a few moments. "But what?"

"That you hated me or something."

Jonah scoffed, baffled. "It's the exact opposite. You were my best friend—you still are. Yeah, it felt different when I saw you at that crime scene because the last time I saw you was at my mother's funeral, but before then...I thought about you all the time. I wondered what big things you were accomplishing down at Quantico, what accolades you might've gotten." He stopped short, shaking his head. "I've missed you every day, and I love you. I just...I guess I couldn't bring myself to say that until now." Now his own eyes were glassy, but he blinked back the tears that threatened to spill.

"I'm so sorry. We should have never avoided each other for this long." Rayne said. "I love you, too."

At that, Jonah gently pulled her back into their embrace, their faces now mere inches apart. Rayne lifted her chin and gave him another thank-you, this one silent—a kiss. A long-awaited one, if Jonah had to admit. It seemed to warm up the brutally cold autumn afternoon almost instantly as they felt their bodies practically melt together, pulling each other in more. The world around them seemed to blur and fade into nothing at all as the kiss deepened, as if nothing else mattered in that moment.

Rayne was the first to break away. "It's cold out here." she visibly shivered.

Jonah couldn't help but let out a small chuckle. "Well, the temperature is dropping by the hour. You shouldn't be out in this weather with those clothes you're wearing, and neither should your dad. Here." He started to shrug off his jacket.

"No, no, that's alright. My house isn't that far from here, I'll be fine."

"Let me drive you and Owen to your house. I can request around-the-clock security when we get there."

"Good idea." Rayne walked around to the other ambulance, where the EMTs were closing the doors, preparing to leave the scene. "Dad? Are you okay?"

"Yes, I'm just fine, my dear. But, are you okay, though?"

"A little shaken up, but I'll be okay. I'm just worried about you. Jonah and I are taking you to my condo until your house is fixed. It looks to me like just the living room and kitchen were damaged. There'll be an agent guarding the door 24/7." She took her father's arm and guided him to Jonah's truck. "When Mom wakes up, she'll stay with you at my place until we catch this guy."

"Speaking of your mother," Owen said as Jonah helped him into the back of the Jeep and fastened his seat belt for him. "The doctor says she could wake up at any time now. When was the last time you've seen her?"

"Not too long ago, but I'll go again in the morning." Rayne said. She turned to Jonah. "Do you think we can get security at her door at the hospital, too?"

"That shouldn't be a problem." Jonah replied as he hopped in on the driver's side and started the engine. Rayne got in the passenger seat beside him. "Who knows what else this man is capable of?"

• • •

Just a few moments later, they were at Rayne's condominium. Rayne and Jonah aided Owen as they walked into the building and took the elevator up to her floor. They made sure he was comfortable on the couch before Rayne turned on the local news on her newly bought flatscreen television, and Jonah phoned the field office to request two available agents, one to guard Owen here at the condo, the second to guard Neevah's hospital room.

"I saw the news van pulling in as we were getting in the car." Rayne explained her reasoning for putting on that specific news channel as she stepped into the kitchen to make her father a batch of tea. "They're already reporting on what happened."

"Looks like they're not saying much." Jonah said, following her into the kitchen. "Bex probably told them to back off."

"Yeah, we don't need any more rumors or false information to start circulating around town. Our culprit's ego is probably already blown up as it is. Do you need anything? Water? Juice?"

"No, I'm fine, thanks."

After preparing the tea, she turned to face him. "Can you come with me to the hospital in the morning? I also need your help with something after."

"Of course. What is it?"

"I'll tell you tomorrow."

• • •

Jonah left Rayne and her father back at her home. It was even colder outside now, the sun starting to dip below an orange and pink horizon. Back at the scene, Sawyer was still conducting an interview with the taxi driver, who was now a key witness. Police were still lingering around, one speaking with Bex and another warding off news crews and nosy neighbors. He walked up to the officer that was talking to Bex.

194

"Did you find him?" Jonah asked. The officer shook his head dismally.

"There's no sign of the suspect anywhere. But Bex says your agents are going to look over Canobie Commons' security footage to see what direction he went after your pursuit with him. I'll send out a few of my own officers to patrol the surrounding neighborhoods."

"Okay. Thank you for coming in a timely manner."

"Anytime, Detective." The officer then shook hands with him and Bex before turning around and leaving.

"That was good judgement on your call, Davenport. I am impressed." Bex stated. "How'd you know this was going to happen?"

He shrugged. "Honestly, I don't know. I just had a weird feeling that something was going to go wrong, and that Owen's discharge from the hospital wasn't going to go smoothly. With the diversion across town turning up with no body and being the same time as his scheduled discharge, I wanted to be safe rather than sorry and beat Owen to his house. Turns out my gut was right."

20

"WE KNOW YOU'VE BEEN WITHHOLDING INFORMATION from us, Simone. Now, you are currently facing charges of being an accomplice to murder and conspiracy." She knew the charges she'd listed were pretty extreme and wouldn't actually stick in a courtroom, but Bex needed her to start talking, and quick. "If you cooperate, we might just let you off the hook. Now, I'm going to ask you again: do you know these two people?"

Simone wailed. After spending one cold, lonely night in the city jail with no food, water, or so much as a sink to clean her face with her skincare products or brush and floss her teeth, her emotions were running high. She was used to the pampered lifestyle, not being a jailbird. She still had on the outfit she wore yesterday when she was arrested, her makeup smeared across her face. "Accomplice to murder? That's absurd! I was set up."

"Ray and Toussaint are already retrieving the online security feed from her estate and surrounding houses that will prove her innocence if she wasn't the one who planted that methanol in her shed, but I want to get her to talk as much as possible first." Bex had told Leigh that morning before stepping into the interrogation room, who'd nodded in agreement.

"We know that she knows the victims." Leigh stated. "If Owen knows them and claims that his wife does too, then his sister-in-law definitely has something to do with them also."

Now in front of Simone, Bex slid the two black and white headshots of Evan Brentwood and Patrice Latimore closer to her. "Who were they to you?"

Simone sighed, realizing that she wasn't going to get out of this. Even if her lawyer was present, the truth was going to come out sooner or later. "Evan wasn't just a radio producer; he was also editing a very special film project. Neevah and I oversaw everything, and Patrice also played a part in making it..."

"Which was...?" Bex prodded.

"It was a film—a documentary, about the Humble Creek Arsonist and how he changed my family's lives forever."

"Similar to your memoir?"

"Well, my book is more about my own life before he started stalking me and my family, and how I made a successful life for myself after that trauma. My fans have been requesting I write one for years."

"You've changed your life by becoming a life coach and speaker, correct?"

"I've gotten to travel all across the globe to speak to other young women and men who are trying to move on from their own horrors. People pay me thousands just to make appearances and host events and conferences now. I even started up my own charity organization...I know this may sound crazy, but if it wasn't for that psychopath almost taking my life, I wouldn't be where I am today."

Bex nodded. "Did you know either of them personally?"

"No, but I've done some research on them before we started filming, and they both had great work in their respective careers. It still doesn't feel real, that they're gone."

"But you do know who killed them, and who tried to kill your sister and brother-in-law?"

"I have a feeling who did it, but I'm not one hundred percent certain."

"I need a name."

"Jason. Jason Flannery." Simone said confidently. "But, he's elusive. Smart, deceptive, he carefully calculated everything he did. And he had quite a few connections throughout the town my sister and I grew up in. He left a single fingerprint at the scene of his last crime which police were able to identify as his, but he vanished right after that, like he knew he'd made a rookie mistake as a murderer and couldn't afford to be captured. He's been off the grid for two decades. No one can find him." Her eyes now had a faraway look, as if she was seeing memories of the past.

"Well, there has to be one place where he hides out at. It could be right where we least expect it. Because he is here. He's killed, and he'll kill again if we don't stop him for good. So think of anywhere, anywhere at all, that he could be at right now that maybe the police had missed years ago."

Simone sucked in a deep breath and let it out slowly, thinking. Then she shuddered.

"The barn..."

•••

It was still a gloomy and dreary day the next morning with a gray sky and bitter winds, but at least it was no longer raining. Apparently the incoming thunderstorm had unexpectedly changed directions late into the night, making an early departure from the town. Smithson East Hospital was loud and bustling when Jonah and Rayne arrived, but they were able to bypass the usual commotion of the popular medical center as they went straight to the elevator on the main floor and descended upward to the burn recovery unit's floor. They greeted the male FBI agent that stood in front of door in a black suit and sunglasses that hid his eyes, guarding, and entered the dim room.

They sat on either side of Neevah as she laid still in her bed. For a few hours, they watched old movies on the room's outdated TV that was mounted high up on the wall in front of them, with very few words being exchanged. In this kind of environment, there wasn't much to say.

Eventually, Jonah spoke. "You said yesterday that you needed my help with something?"

Rayne didn't meet his gaze, but she did respond. "Yeah. I do. I'm going up to Humble Creek, and I could use some backup."

"You think they have more records on this arsonist guy that we can take a look at?"

"They should have more information than the city does. They have their own police station, so they probably have files on every single event that'd happened there. At least, I hope they do." Rayne said.

"It won't hurt to try." Jonah said. "But, you have to be careful. That maniac that almost ran you off the road, he's most likely still out there, waiting for the perfect moment to strike again. They could very well be the same guy that terrorized our victims."

"Which is why I'm asking you to come with me. With both of us there, nothing will go down, I'm sure."

"We'll need supplies, just in case. We can go down to the field office and I'll grab a few things before we go."

"Good idea."

Just then, a nurse knocked on the door and stepped inside, stating that it was almost time to transport Neevah to get a CT scan, and asked if Rayne or Jonah needed anything. Rayne said no but thank you as she gripped her mother's hand and held it tight. "I hope you wake up soon." she whispered sadly. Moments later, two of Neevah's fingers slowly tightened around her hand, and Rayne gasped.

"Mom? You can hear me, can you? I'm right here. Jonah's here, too. You're safe. Dad is safe at home too." But to her dismay, Neevah let go.

Shortly after, two transporters came and whisked away Neevah and her life support equipment down to a CT scanner, the hired security guard walking quickly behind them. Jonah stood and took Rayne's hand, squeezing it two times.

"Let's go solve this." he said.

• • •

Humble Creek, Pennsylvania was within the county, but it was still a good forty-five minute drive away from Ruxlor City. From Jonah and Rayne's collaborative research, it was a small town in the middle of nowhere, and everybody knew everybody. The population was only 18,000, and Rayne had learned that her mother's high school graduating class only consisted of a little over one hundred students, and each and every one of them stayed rooted in the secluded town they grew up in, minus the Alistair family after their dark encounter with a serial stalker and arsonist. Even though she was considered a celebrity within the town, Neevah hadn't been back since college and had never made Humble Creek a destination during any of her numerous book tours.

The atmosphere was growing mysterious and uncanny as they approached their exit. They passed a faded and weathered mint-green welcome sign and followed the spotty GPS signal to a nearby market. They didn't have very many people to interview today, but they were planning on staying for the entire day and learning as much about the township as they could.

At the local market, Rayne bought a hoagie, bag of chips, and a lemonade from the outdated store, and Jonah grabbed a bottle of flavored water and wafers. Afterward, they drove one mile to the police station, where (hopefully) they would find anyone who could recount what they witnessed all those years ago. It was a far stretch, but it was worth a shot. And sometimes in their line of work, miracles could happen.

The Humble Creek Borough Police Station was only half the size of Ruxlor City's. It was a brown, square building that looked like it had seen better days, but the landscaping looked freshly kept up on and the parking lot recently repaved. Jonah parked the unmarked car he'd checked out from the FBI field office, and the pair headed inside. A middle-aged secretary was sitting at a desk behind a glass wall in the middle of the lobby, and they stopped in front of her.

"Good afternoon, ma'am." Jonah began. "I'm Detective Jonah Davenport and this is Detective Rayne Winters from Ruxlor City FBI, Violent Crimes Unit. Who's your sheriff here?"

The secretary perked up after seeing their badges and hearing where they'd come from. "That would be Sheriff Eddie Douglas, but he's at lunch right now. He won't be back for about a half an hour."

"That's fine. We can wait." Rayne said.

So they waited.

An hour later, just past three o'clock, a tall figure stepped into the waiting area. Sheriff Eddie Douglas. He noticed the agents right away with their professional business-like attire, poised stances, and badges that were pinned to her chests, and he stopped in his tracks. Rayne stood first and went over to introduce herself. Eddie looked to be about six feet tall, mid- to late-fifties or sixties, maybe even older than that, wrinkled skin, and tired blue eyes, fully equipped with handcuffs, taser, a radio, and a nine millimeter semiautomatic pistol. Jonah came prepared with a few tools too if things went left, and since Rayne was technically off the case, all of her gear was confiscated, but she kept her own Glock underneath the driver's seat of the car they borrowed.

"Eddie Douglas, sheriff for the borough of Humble Creek. And whom do I have the pleasure of speaking with?" He glanced at her badge and stuck out his hand.

"Detective Winters, Ruxlor City FBI." Rayne replied as she shook the man's hand. "And that's my partner, Detective Davenport. If you have a moment, we'd just like to ask you a few questions and explain some of the troubles we've been having back in the city. Do you mind?"

"Not at all, Detectives. Please, follow me. My office is straight down here to the right." Sheriff Eddie Douglas nodded, and Rayne and Jonah followed him down to his office. He flicked on a lightswitch, but the bulb flickered a few times before coming on. He sat behind a dusty cherrywood desk, and the duo sat down on a worn sofa beside the door. "So." he folded his hands together on top of his desk. "What brings you all the way to this end of the county? Haven't spoke with an officer from the city in quite some time."

"Well..." Rayne told the story from the beginning, starting with the first murder, up until the alleged diversions that have been happening to distract her team from finding the culprit.

"I do apologize, but...that can't be right. The last time we caught that guy, he almost killed himself escaping and had major injuries. If he even survived his injuries, it would be nearly impossible to pull off those kinds of fires without putting himself in the crosshairs or leaving incriminating evidence that your unit would've picked up on by now. This may be a whole new mastermind that your department is dealing with."

"So, you're saying this could be a copycat...?" Jonah said.

"I would believe that theory, but..." Rayne said, "my mother is one of the recent targets. This is her second time being terrorized by a criminal like this. And, my aunt wrote a memoir about what they went through in this very town. Aside from that, our profilers studied the methods of this guy with the one from the past, and everything matches up exactly, there are no differences. This has to be the same person seeking vengeance or whatever else they have ingrained in their mind, not a copycat finishing what was started decades ago. I came here to see if anyone still remembered anything, or if there's any police reports or archives my partner and I can take a look at."

"Your mother...is she Ms. Neevah Alistair?" Eddie Douglas raised his eyebrows, some memories of one of his very first major cases after being appointed to sherriff coming back to his mind in flashes.

"Yes, she is. Her and my father were the third and fourth victims of a recent attack, but they're alive."

"I'm very sorry to hear that. I read every one of her books. She's like a celebrity around here, even though no one really sees her anymore."

"I appreciate your concern. We're just trying to find who did this and get justice for my parents and the other victims. Do you think you can help?"

"I can try my best." Eddie Douglas got comfortable in his leather office chair. "I was put on that case shortly after I got promoted and made an arrest. My memory is a bit spotty these days, but I still remember everything that went down. It's hard for one to forget the townspeople's hysteria, the media frenzy, the negative stigma it's had on this town ever since. It even made national news for about two or three weeks. Then as quick as it started, it was all over with, and everybody just...moved on."

An eerie silence filled the small room, and Jonah cleared his throat. "Well, to start, do you have any case files, police reports, or notes we can borrow?"

"I don't see why not. No one's had to use them in decades. Our archives are stored downstairs on the basement level. You can take the elevator in the lobby." Eddie said.

"Thank you, Sheriff." At that, Jonah and Rayne stood and navigated their way downstairs to a storage-like facility where archives, cold case files, and other important records were kept. As they took a few minutes to search, Rayne was already pleased with how their investigation was going here.

"There was nothing useful for us back in the city." Rayne told Jonah as she pulled out several manila folders and set them down on a nearby steel table. She opened one and skimmed over it. "We can drive by these addresses and see if anything is worth looking into, then interview civilians who were witnesses that are still living here."

"Sounds like a plan. This guy is hiding somewhere, and we won't stop until he's found again. He could be right under our noses, for all we know."

They collected what they needed and reshelved everything else exactly as they'd found it before leaving the station. But as they came closer to their car, they could immediately sense that something was off. They climbed in and Jonah started the engine, but the orange low fuel light flashed at him.

"Impossible. I filled up this tank before we left." Jonah muttered annoyedly.

"Maybe there's a gas leak somewhere?" Rayne inquired.

"That would be highly unlikely; this car was just inspected a couple weeks ago. The agent told me before I rented it out. And the pavement looked pretty dry when we were walking up to it. I guess I'll just have to fill up again..."

They ventured five miles to a local gas station, where Jonah used a gas card to fill up the agency-issued vehicle once more.

While he did that, Rayne determined the first address they were going to head to.

A barn.

21

THE OLD, ABANDONED FARMLAND EXTENDED FOR several miles, with nothing but scenic, even peaceful rolling plains dotted with a few crumbling farmhouses and sheds here and there. But one large red barn stuck out like a sore thumb on top of a hill that was the size of a mountaintop.

That was where Rayne wanted to go first.

"Are you sure there's anything up here?" Jonah said as the little sedan slowly chugged up the hill with protest. There were no roads, just dead yellowed grass that was muddied from the previous days of heavy rains. "I know people were speculating about this place but never searched it, but that was over twenty years ago. The place looks like it's probably one more storm away from crumbling down to pieces."

"I'm positive." Rayne answered. "After the research we did, I'm confident that something is still here. If not hard evidence, then at least a clue that'll take us in the right direction."

Jonah didn't say anything else as they crept closer to the barn. When they were about a few yards away and the hill gradually became less steep, he put the gear into Park and pulled up the emergency brake before killing the engine.

Once again, the low fuel light blinked back at them.

"Maybe someone was tampering with the car? While we were talking to the sheriff?" Rayne wondered aloud.

"We'll have to check the station's security feed when we're done with this. Whoever decided to tamper with an FBI vehicle is going to be facing some serious charges, and they'll regret it. Let's hurry so we can get back to the station and file a report."

"Good idea."

They got out of the car, leaving the files inside on the back seat. But just then, they heard a faint sound in the distance—as if someone was closing a creaky door. Jonah turned and squinted at a weathered and decayed white farmhouse that laid a few dozen yards away.

"There might still be people living there." he said. "I'm gonna go check it out, you wait here and watch the car. Do you have your gun?"

She patted her holster that was hidden underneath her jacket. "Yeah, I got it."

"Okay. I'll be back in a few minutes."

She watched him leave.

When he was out of sight, she turned around and headed into the barn.

But, to her disappointment, the five thousand-square-foot structure was dark and barren. Piles of hay bales were stacked in one corner, with common trash like cigarette butts and empty beer cans, and shards of broken glass crackled under her boots. While it had a few makeshift rooms constructed with bare drywall, it looked like the space was uninhabited aside from the occasional underage party. Whatever evidence had been here was probably long since destroyed. But Rayne took pictures of most of the interior of the barn anyway with her cell phone so she could go back and analyze them later before turning and walking out. She checked her watch as she strolled back down to the sedan. It was around three o'clock, but the sky was already starting to turn into a beautiful shade of pink and baby blue, the bright white sun beginning to dip below the horizon, shining down on the cold autumn day.

But as she approached the car, that same uncanny feeling made her stomach drop again, and her breath hitch in her throat.

All four tires had been slashed, the air quickly depleting with a high-pitched hiss.

What...? But before she could register any thoughts, something heavy bashed into the back of her skull, sending a searing pain throughout her entire body.

Everything went black.

• • •

Jonah had been knocking on the battered screen door with a balled fist for about twenty minutes. He didn't have a search warrant, so he couldn't simply enter someone's home as he pleased and demanded people start talking. He'd sworn he and Rayne heard the sound of a door slamming shut, and that it had to have come from this house; this was the closest residence from the barn and looked the most well-kept.

Rayne!

He'd been gone too long. He had to get back to the barn and accompany Rayne, who he knew was bent on finding something—anything—that would bring them closer to finding the truth and avenging the victims, closing this case for good. She couldn't be alone for too long, not in this kind of setting. He shook his head as he went down the wooden porch steps and started his trek back in the direction that he'd came from. But as the car came back into view, he stopped suddenly in his tracks and pulled out his gun from its holster in one swift motion.

The tires were slashed.

Who did this?

"Rayne? *Rayne!*" Jonah called out. "Where are you?" But he got no response, his voice echoing in the great open plains.

He cursed under his breath as he took the gun off of safety mode and ran into the darkness of the barn...

• • •

Her eyes slowly fluttered open as she came back into consciousness. However, her vision was blurred, so her eyes couldn't focus on anything for a few moments. Goosebumps covered her bare shoulders and arms, and her whole body shivered. Rayne realized she was no longer wearing her jacket, only the plain white V-necked shirt that she'd had on underneath it. Did she take it off? Or did someone else?

She was sitting upright, in a chair, but when she attempted to stand up, she couldn't—she was stuck. No, she was trapped, her wrists bound behind the chair with thick rope and her ankles bound to the leg posts.

Help! Help! Her mind was screaming the words, but she couldn't open her mouth to physically speak them; duct tape tightly covered her lips. *Of course I'm silenced—I've been abducted*, she thought angrily. *Where am I? Am I still at the barn?*

Oh, no—Jonah! Where is he?

As her vision finally started to adjust, Rayne saw that she was, in fact, still inside the old barn, in one of the makeshift rooms made of thin drywall and the floor made of grass and straw. Fear paralyzed her as her eyes fell upon a tall, dark figure standing in the doorway. He was holding what looked like a large bottle, but Rayne wasn't too sure. The room she was in was dim with very little sunlight shining through the barn's crumbling roof. Pretty soon, the sun would be dipping below the horizon, and there wouldn't be any light at all...

But just as quickly as she noticed the figure's presence, he was gone. Her eyes darted around the room, heart beating rapidly in her chest, but she was alone. Then she heard feet shuffling somewhere, and she assumed it was the same person she just saw.

Or were there several of them?

Several seconds that felt like minutes unbearably passed before Rayne heard a faint sound of liquid being poured into a container. She then heard what she believed was someone lighting a match. What was being done? If only she knew.

She smelled fire.

• • •

"Rayne! Rayne, can you hear me? Where are you?" Jonah frantically looked around, but he didn't see her—

WHACK!

Something hard and ice-cold slammed against his temple, and Jonah cried out in pain as he stumbled backward and gripped the front of his head with both his hands.

"I'm the one you've been hunting." a low voice said somewhere in the darkness, but Jonah's head was spinning, and he couldn't pinpoint where it was coming from. "I'm the one your team claims to have been so close to catching. This ends here and now."

"Who are you?" Jonah yelled out as he stood up straight, head throbbing. "Where's Rayne?"

"If you must know, Detective: the name's Jason." The figure—Jason—swung the pipe again, this time striking Jonah right in the stomach, causing him to collapse to the ground and hug his torso in agony.

"How do you know who I am?" Jonah yelled, grimacing through the pain.

"I know everything about you, Davenport. I've done some research on you and your sidekick over the past week. You're a pretty good rookie, but you're not good enough..." The pipe hit the back of his knees with a hard crack, demobilizing him. "In about five minutes, this whole place is going to erupt, with both of you in it. Even bigger than that explosion I set off in Ruxlor, I might add. No one will find you..."

Little did this guy know, Jonah had dialed 911 just before running into the barn. But would they come in time? Would they even find them here? Or would they be checking the wrong locations? He only had a few seconds to yell into his phone to come to the abandoned farmland ASAP before hanging up and rushing inside. Would enough backup come so they could capture this criminal once and for all?

Jason swung the pipe once more, crashing down on Jonah's arm, sending a searing pain throughout his elbow, shoulder, and left side of his body, and he cried out. He was becoming weaker from the intense blows to his head, stomach, and arm, unable to move or try to defend himself from this madman. He said his 'sidekick' would parish inside the barn too. Did he mean Rayne? Did she experience the same torture as himself—or worse? He couldn't fathom the thought of her being hit like he was right now, and he pushed the thought away, but it lingered in the back of his mind. He was on the right side of the law, but if this guy had severely injured Rayne, or worse, killed her, Jonah would no doubt make him pay for what he did, whether he was arrested today or not. But right now, the only thing on his mind was survival as Jason, who was satisfied seeing the FBI agent curled up on the ground, became preoccupied with something else a few feet away in the corner of the barn, and a strong scent filled Jonah's nose and made his eyes water. Methanol.

Jonah's ears were ringing, but he still managed to speak. "You...you set her up, didn't you? Simone never knew she had methanol at her home—you planted it there so she would take the fall for all of this, and not you."

Jason didn't respond. Actually, he ignored him altogether, putting the finishing touches on his masterpiece with his back turned, before lighting a tiny match and dropping it into a large bucket. It glowed orange on the inside, but it didn't blow up, at least not yet.

Luckily, Jonah heard loud police sirens in the distance, and he closed his eyes and whispered a small prayer of relief. Jason cursed and pulled a small handgun that had been in his back pants pocket. He checked the ammunition before aiming it at the entryway of the barn.

"Police! You're surrounded!" a deep voice boomed from outside.

"In here!" Jonah called out, praying that they could hear him. "Hurry! Time's running out! It's a trap!"

A troupe of six officers stormed the building, stopping behind Jonah and aiming their weapons directly at Jason.

"Are you okay, kid?" one older male officer said, glancing down at him.

"I'll be okay." Jonah said, but he was still succumbing to the pain. "But Rayne, she's my partner, a detective, she's still in here. I have to find her before this place goes up in flames." He mustered up just enough strength to get back on his feet, but the pain that coursed through his body felt almost unbearable. But he couldn't give up. Not until he found her and got her out of here. "He says that in five minutes, this barn will erupt into flames. We all need to get out of here, now."

"Drop your weapon." another officer commanded. "It's over, Flannery. You're under arrest."

While the officers were slowly circling around Jason Flannery, Jonah limped around the rest of the barn in a frantic search for Rayne. He found an open doorway and stepped through it, and relief flooded through him.

"Rayne!" He wanted to run to her, but his left knee was beginning to swell, so he could only limp over. He gently pulled off the duct tape that covered her mouth, and Rayne coughed.

"Jonah! Thank god you're alive. I'm so sorry, we should've never split up." Rayne began to cry.

"There's no time for apologies right now. We have less than five minutes before this place explodes. Police have our suspect surrounded now. I'm gonna get you out of here—"

Just then, a series of gunshots rang out behind them, causing them both to flinch, and Jonah had a feeling that Jason Flannery had fired shots first, causing the officers to fire back.

"Did you get hurt? You look awful." Rayne said as Jonah painstakingly crouched behind her and tried to get a grip on the rope behind the chair that kept her arms bound together.

"Just a little banged up, but it's not a big deal." he lied. When he was finally able to untie the first of two tight knots, thick gray smoke began to fill the air.

"We're almost out of time, aren't we?" he heard her whisper.

"Don't worry, we're getting out of this alive. I'll make sure of it." He didn't know what was going on in the room beside them, if the police had successfully gotten custody of their suspect or not, but the only thing that mattered to him right now was saving Rayne. The smoke stung their eyes and irritated their lungs, causing them to struggle. A few seconds that felt like an eternity later, Rayne's hands were freed. "Hurry. You untie one foot, I'll get the other one." Jonah said breathlessly as he scrambled to get ahold of another piece of rope. They worked together hecticly as the temperature in the room started to heat up, making them sweat, and their clothes sticking to their skin.

When the rope was finally untied, Rayne's body ached from being bound to the chair for so long, but she mentally pushed the pain aside as she wrapped one arm around Jonah and helped him out of the room.

Neither one could see very far ahead of them; now, a crackling fire had begun in the large container Jonah had seen Jason Flannery filling up earlier that illuminated the space, and was the source of the impending explosion. The officers were gone, and so was Jason. No one was here, except for them. Jonah could feel that he was weighing Rayne down as they slowly walked across the room, and he forced himself to not feel guilty about her holding him up as they made a slow but sure escape.

They took one step out of the door and into the sun.

And everywhere around them went up into flames.

EPILOGUE

1 Month Later

SNOWFLAKES HAD BEEN FALLING FOR MOST of the day, covering Ruxlor City in a thick white blanket. The FBI Field Office was busy as usual, with operations going on left and right despite the incoming holiday season. Crime didn't stop for anything, and neither did the dedicated agents of the Violent Crimes unit.

But today, some of them had a well-deserved day off.

"Jonah, could you turn off the oven for me and check on the pies?" Lacey called from the powder room in the hallway, where she was adjusting her makeup before their guests arrived.

Jonah went into the kitchen to check on the food. It was Thanksgiving Day, one of many holidays that he normally struggled with since the loss of his mother, but for the first this year, the heavy weight of grief didn't drag him down or fog his mind. Instead, he was actually beginning to feel a tiny spark of happiness in his heart again, along with hope for the future.

Ding-dong, the doorbell echoed.

Because of who was at the door.

"I got it." Jonah told his father Sam and Lacey, who were now finishing prepping the dinner table, and he finished setting the freshly baked pumpkin pies on the stove before walking over to the front door and opening it.

There stood Rayne, holding a box of lemon cakes from the local bakery, and his heart swelled up with joy. Behind her were her parents, Neevah and Owen, hand in hand. Neevah had awoken from her coma shortly after the capture of Jason Flannery, but she was still a bit weak and used a cane for balance, and Rayne took her and Owen to physical therapy three times a week after work. Their bandages were still present but covered up with their coats.

"Owen! Neevah! We are so grateful and overjoyed that you guys could make it. Here, let me help you to the table." Lacey appeared and guided Rayne's parents down the hall and to the dining room.

"I'll take those off your hands." Sam said happily, and Rayne handed the box of sweets over to him to put in the kitchen.

The pair embraced warmly. When they separated, they were both smiling.

"I still can't believe we closed our first case over a month ago." Rayne spoke first.

"And Bex already assigned us to our second." Jonah added. "Pretty soon we should both be able to move up the ranks in the division."

"Are you sure you should be putting weight on your leg?" Rayne questioned, motioning to the brace on his left leg.

"Doc said it's fine now." he assured her, although he knew she could tell he was favoring his right leg more than his left.

Rayne thought about the brutal injuries he had sustained the day they'd arrested Jason Flannery. "You saved my life back there."

"I know; you remind me every day." he chuckled.

"And you saved my father's life, too. I'll never be able to thank you enough for that."

"I suppose I did, but without your determination and persistence, we wouldn't have had the right resources and evidence to have been able to catch our culprit and stop all that chaos. I don't want to take all the credit for ending this; we both took him down. Together."

"You're right. We make a pretty good team."

"We do."

"Hopefully we get some traction with this current assignment. We need leads but nobody's talking."

"I know. It's going to get tough again, but we'll worry about that tomorrow. Today we're taking a break from being FBI agents. Today, we're just us."

She smiled. "Just us."

Hand in hand, they walked together to join their families.

THE END

DISCUSSION QUESTIONS

1. Character Motivations: How do the two rookie FBI agents' personal histories—Rayne's parents being targeted and Jonah's mother's death—shape their decisions and emotional responses throughout the investigation?

2. Trust & Partnership: In what ways does the intense pressure of their first major case strengthen or strain the relationship between Jonah and Rayne? Did you feel their partnership developed naturally?

3. Ethical Gray Areas: Were there moments when either agent crossed ethical or procedural lines due to personal stakes? Were their choices justified?

4. Home as a Battleground: What impact does the arsonist targeting Rayne's parents have on the story's tension? How does this threat to "home" deepen the suspense?

5. Villain Complexity: Does the serial arsonist have a compelling motive or psychological profile? How does the author balance mystery with revealing clues about the antagonist?

6. Themes of Inexperience vs. Instinct: How does the agents' rookie status affect their approach to solving the case? Do they rely more on instinct, training, or emotional drive?

7. Pacing & Suspense: Which moments or chapters were the most suspenseful, and how did the pacing contribute to the escalating danger?

8. Resolution & Justice: Did the ending provide satisfying answers about the arsonist's motives and the agents' personal arcs? What questions, if any, were intentionally left unresolved?

1

"WHO IS SHE?"

"We don't know. She's not saying anything."

"Where did she come from?"

"She was found outside of Bayview Park. No one's claimed her either. She's so young, she must have family, right?"

"What happened?"

"It's hard to say. But looking at her, she's terrified. But she won't tell us anything—"

A knock on her cubicle wall pulled her out of her thoughts. Toni Lee looked up to see Lieutenant Jack Owens, their shift commander for the day, looking down at her with concern.

"You alright, Lee?" Owens said, eyebrows furrowed.

Toni rubbed her temples with her fingers then continued to type on her computer. "I'm good, sir, thank you." She admired his gold shoulder boards that displayed his rank; her goal was to become a lieutenant one day, maybe even captain or chief. But until then, she had to work her way up, and pay her dues as a detective.

Owens nodded. "I've got orders from Sandstone. He got a call to a scene, and he assigned you to it. He wants you there ASAP."

Barry Sandstone was the captain of their department's detectives bureau, and one of their bosses. He was underneath the chief of police, but nonetheless ran their division smoothly and made sure the Chief's orders were being carried out in an efficient manner. Toni nodded and signed out of her desktop computer. She was fairly new to the homicide unit, and was eager to be the first assigned to this new case. "Of course. Do they have a report?" She slid on her peacoat and grabbed the key to the unmarked cruiser she usually drove while on duty.

"Female, late twenties, estimated to be missing for about two weeks and reported ten days ago. She was found in the woodlands near the county line just an hour ago. No criminal history or known criminal relations, she comes from a high-up family. No outer marks but there are signs of struggle. That's all I've got from the report. Sergeant Maxwell will assist you when you get there. I just texted you the location."

"Who else got assigned to it?"

"Just you."

She paused. "Just me?"

Owens nodded.

"But . . ." *Am I ready for this?* "I've only been working in homicide for about a year. We're a small borough, our department shouldn't be overloaded with cases. I don't have a secondary officer on this one?"

The lieutenant shrugged. "You'll have to take that up with Sandstone. But you're right, everyone in the bureau right now is more than able to take on another case with their current workload. This sounds like a pretty rough case, in my opinion."

Toni knew she had to stay confident if she wanted to prove herself to her superiors, so she tried to shake the uneasy feeling she had as she headed out of the office, thanking the lieutenant on her way out.

Vaughn Black had a feeling that there was going to be more entailed to this job than Bex was letting on.

But nonetheless, he went with it.

"So, let me get this straight . . ." he rubbed his face with his hand, his other hand holding his cell phone up to his ear. "All I have to do is accompany a detective with a homicide? Not run the investigation or make any decisions, just be an assistant? Taking up space?"

"Precisely!" Assistant Special Agent-in-Charge Bex Chapman's enthusiastic voice didn't sway him, but he let her continue. "As usual, you'll have access to all of our resources and databases, and whenever she or her department needs them, they'll have you to access them. You will be relieved of your duties when they make an arrest."

He pondered for a moment. It was an easy enough job, and at the moment he didn't feel as if he was ready to jump straight into profiling work or fieldwork again. Playing assistant to a detective in a small town wouldn't cause any harm, would it?

"What department did you say? Casper?"

"Yes. Their unit is small but recently renovated, but they've informed me that they'd feel better if they had backup from federal on this; they haven't dealt with a murder case in a long time." Casper was a quaint lake beach town that was identified as a borough, just forty-five minutes away from Ruxlor City. From what Vaughn knew, the little town's police department had an impressive budget and was backed by the sheriff's department for certain issues, so why did they request Bex and her FBI team for just one case?

"Tell them I accept. When do I start?"

"Actually, they need you on the scene now."

* * *

He was back in the line of fire. Not right now, but he would be soon enough.

Now, Vaughn wore his faded but cherished navy blue windbreaker that displayed the letters *FBI* on the back in bold yellow letters, khaki pants and muddied boots, trekking through dark woodlands as he made his way to the location Bex had sent him.

He had resigned from the FBI two years ago, down to the very day. And now he was back. A moment later, he came upon a clearing in the woods, and from the spectacle that he saw before him, he knew he had arrived at the scene.

He looked around. It was early afternoon but the leaves of the hundreds of red oaks around him blocked the sunlight, making it look like dusk. The dimness gave off an uncanny feeling, but he ignored his paranoia as his boss, Bex Chapman, appeared alongside her right-hand woman, Supervisory Special Agent Leigh Crenshaw, who was also a criminal psychologist by trade. With Vaughn, there was one more criminal profiler on their team, Roscoe Hall, and one profiler-in-training, Rayne Winters. They had two detectives, Jonah Davenport and Diana Reeves, one forensics specialist, Sawyer Blackridge, and two technical liaisons, Anisa Ray and Keon Toussaint. Together

233

they made up what was now called the Joint Operations Task Force.

"It's good to have you back, Black." Relief flooded Leigh's voice as she firmly shook Vaughn's hand.

Vaughn nodded his appreciation. His team had been practically pleading for him to return over the last two years, but their pleas had fallen on deaf ears. Well, until Bex called him with a "special" job that was really meant to coax him back into his job.

"Don't worry, we'll throw you a nice welcome-back party for coming back on such short notice." Bex patted his shoulder, but her short stature had trouble reaching up to his six-foot-four frame.

Leigh got right to it. "We know you're not leading this one, but take a look around and see if you spot anything out of the ordinary. Both our people and the borough's swept the perimeter from top to bottom, but there's no signs of anyone else being here. You, however, may think otherwise."

Vaughn started to walk slowly, his boots crunching on twigs and crisp leaves on the ground. He still wondered how the bureau got dragged into a potentially open-and-shut case?

Well, he would have to ask the detective in charge that question.

"Where is the detective I'll be assisting?" he asked, still surveying the grim scene.

"There." Bex motioned over to the crime scene technicians who were doing their best to collect any traces of evidence they could find. "Over there talking to CSI, in the knit sweater."

Vaughn caught sight of the detective and quickly trekked to the other end of the clearing. But as soon as he got close enough to see her . . .

"Toni?"

The detective looked up from her notepad, and their gazes locked.

"Vaughn?"

"This is your case?" He stopped just a few inches away from her. "You're a detective now."

The corners of her doe-brown eyes crinkled when she gave a small smile. "I am, actually. And you are . . . ?"

"Apparently I'm your new liaison."

"Hm." she hummed, looking him up and down. She spotted his badge. "You're FBI?"

"My sixth year. I'm with the field office in the city, in a task force for Violent Crimes. My boss and your boss put this partnership together, and I'm here until you make an arrest."

"I see." Toni Lee quickly broke their gaze and glanced toward the white sheet that covered the body.

He hadn't seen her in what felt like an eternity. Her surprise was mutual; the last time they saw one another, it was at the end of their police academy training. It seems they both had achieved their goals and more . . . but, would everything that they left in the past be brought into the present?

Neither of them could think about that now. Not with a dead woman just mere feet away from them.

2

"**I KNOW THE SIGNIFICANCE OF** our UNSUB of leaving the victim here." Toni Lee stated, handing Vaughn copies of notes and profiles from her department regarding the UNSUB—the unknown subject.

"And you guys are one hundred percent sure these cases are related?" Vaughn skimmed through the notes, not yet convinced just from the papers alone.

"I'm sure." she said, confidence in her voice. "This is the final place the search party for Jane Blystone, the victim, was looking before she turned up here today. To him, this is a game."

"This definitely is a sick version of a game." Vaughn said as he browsed through the profiles of all of the victims and closed the manila folder. He was eager to get back into his cubicle and do a deep dive into the cases. "He does this for fun. This woman doesn't have any visible connections to the previous victims? But your department is absolutely certain this is by the same person?"

Toni shook her head. "No similarities except for age, gender and body type. And he knew that we would be here—he left a note written to my department beside her body, like he did for his previous victims. One of the techs is swabbing it for fingerprints now. The motive? We have no idea, yet."

Vaughn took in all of this information, jotting it down in his notebook. He would make more in-depth notes when he was back at headquarters, then accompany Toni in creating a game plan on how they were going to catch the UNSUB for good.

Toni gave the crime scene techs permission to release the scene, that way they could get everything processed down at the laboratory as soon as possible. The techs began to take down the yellow crime scene tape, and everyone was on the same page as to what needed to be done next. As she gave out orders, Vaughn couldn't help but take in her presence. She looked exactly the same, just slightly older, and the academy seemed to have successfully broken her out of her shell. At least that he knew of. Her long, curly auburn hair was now cut into a short pixie cut but still complimented her oval-shaped face and striking hazel eyes. A shining gold badge was clipped to her blue turtleneck, and she wore black dress pants and ballet flats, which were already dirtied from the sloshy grass. He could tell by her outfit that she was a Casper resident, not accustomed to the woodlands that surrounded the rest of the county. She was dressed for the lake or the beach or the boardwalk. But even Casper, and its beach Casper Bay, wasn't perfect. Crime was everywhere, but it appeared Toni Lee meant business.

Bex and Leigh walked up to the duo.

"I just got off the phone with Casper's mayor." Bex informed them. "He wants a press conference Sunday morning at nine a.m. for the morning news."

"Sunday morning? That's tomorrow." Toni said. Vaughn could tell by her voice that she was nervous. Was this her first case? Or was something else rattling her nerves? "We didn't even have time to confirm that Jane Blystone's murder is related to the others. Our evidence may not even be done processing until Monday afternoon, if not even a few days later. My department's lab is small, and we have other cases that are still taking precedence right now."

"That's exactly what I tried to explain to him, but he's adamant on making a statement and us being there. Apparently Jane was a local celebrity of sorts."

"She wasn't that much of a celebrity." Toni scoffed. "Her father owns quite a few commercial properties in our area, but he's just a businessman who happened to get rich."

"But that could point us in the direction of a motive." Vaughn stated. "I'm not sure about the others, but I have a feeling that once I fully dive into these cases, something will come up that can show us what direction we need to take."

"If you're not comfortable speaking at the press conference, our team will handle it." Leigh said to Toni. "This isn't fair to you that you were just assigned this case today and they want you to put yourself in front of a potentially very angry public in just mere hours. Our team is more experienced and prepared for anything. I'll call everyone in and we can swap notes and be ready to take this thing head on by morning."

"Thank you." Toni shook her head in disbelief. "You all are lifesavers. Now I see why my boss called you in to help me. Your team must do amazing work."

"Eh, we have a few tricks up our sleeves." Bex grinned. "But I do have a superbly talented squad that does everything in their power to get justice. Whatever you need, Detective Lee, please don't hesitate to ask Agent Black. He will be your in-between for your guys and the JOTF."

"I appreciate that very much."

During their conversation, the sun had begun to dip below the horizon; their source of light was almost completely gone, and the trees certainly didn't help the remaining amount of sunlight that tried to shine through their leaves.

"It's getting dark. I'll call the rest of the team in." Leigh said. "Let's meet at headquarters at eight a.m. sharp. Everyone okay with that?"

"Good idea. I don't want to be out here any longer than necessary." Toni replied, in which Vaughn thought was odd for a detective of her caliber.

He had his own reason for feeling uneasy in the dark woods.

What was hers?

* * *

Vaughn helped Toni avoid puddles of mud and wet grass as they trekked back toward the entrance of the woods. They moved at a snail's pace, and Bex and Leigh were already way ahead of them.

"So, how long have you been in the police force?" he asked as they walked at a slow pace. He held out his arm for her just in case she tripped or slipped.

"Not long." Toni answered. "After graduating from the academy, I spent five years as an officer before I was finally promoted to detective. I spent my first year in our missing persons unit, but not a lot goes on over there. This past year I transferred to homicide. How long have you been doing this for?"

"After the academy and college, I went straight to Quantico for FBI training. I applied to work for the Ruxlor City field office, and I've been here ever since as a special agent. During all those years I've been working towards becoming a profiler, and three years ago I finally got the promotion I wanted. And now, here I am."

"Impressive."

Soon enough, they arrived at the dead-end dirt road that led back to the main entrance of the woods and then into town, where their cars were parked in a line. Bex and Leigh usually drove to scenes together, and their agency-issued vehicle was already gone. They had to assemble the Joint Operations Task Force and collect every file pertaining to the cases that were believed to be linked to this one in less than two hours, thanks to one mayor's impatience.

Vaughn was about to cross the street over to the other side of the wide road, but stayed put when he noticed there were three cars parked instead of two. The CSI van and the coroner's van had left way before them, and no one else was in the woodlands now. Or was there?

A battered, dark colored SUV was parked further down the road. With the depleting sunlight he couldn't tell what color it was, he guessed dark blue or black, nor whether or not a driver was occupying it. Maybe it's just a hiker's or volunteer's, he thought to himself. But who would be hiking or picking up litter this late in the day? His own red Tahoe sat behind a polished, cream colored Chrysler 300, which he made the easy guess that it belonged to Toni. She retrieved her key fob, which displayed the Chrysler logo, and began walking to her car. Was he just being paranoid?

When Toni was halfway across, the SUV's blinding high beams came on, and it suddenly sprang forward. It seemed to accelerate at lightning speed, barreling towards her.

"Toni!"

He didn't waste any time as he jumped into action, running out into the middle of the road and tackling her, and they both rolled into the grass.

The SUV came to a screeching halt upon realizing that it had missed its target, but when Vaughn sprang back up, now aiming his Max-9 pistol at the truck, it made a harsh U-turn, almost flipping itself over, and sped away. He fired two shots, trying to take out the back tires, but it was no use.

The SUV was gone.

Toni coughed as dust and debris from the road swirled around her, and she wiped the dirt off of her pants and the sleeves of her sweater, even though she knew her outfit was ruined. Her thin knit sweater had ripped, and she now had a bloody scrape on her right elbow.

She made an attempt to stand on her own, but Vaughn immediately stepped in. "No, allow me to help. I'm the one that pushed you." He took hold of her waist and easily lifted her up onto her feet. "Are you alright?"

"I think so, but . . . W-Who was that?"

"I don't know." He answered as he looked into the distance, still holding onto her. Their gazes locked. "But why did they come after you?"

Toni quickly broke their gaze. "I don't know."

ABOUT THE AUTHOR

BONNIE SYNCLAIRE is an award-winning author of mystery, thriller and suspense novels where love, danger, and buried truths collide. Her novels center resilient women forced into reckoning moments—by cold cases, family secrets, corruption or loss—where survival depends as much on emotional courage as physical strength. Set against cinematic backdrops like coastal towns, hospitals, courtrooms and storm-scarred towns, her stories blend slow-burn romance with high-stakes mystery and thriller momentum.

Her love for storytelling garnered her numerous short fiction literature awards at a young age, including a state title. She published her debut novel in print at 16, being featured in the Pittsburgh Tribune-Review, Saturday Light Brigade Radio and others. Her books have been sold in Australia, Germany, Japan, Great Britain and the United States. A prolific writer, ghostwriter and editor, she was nominated to be included in Marquis Publications' *Who's Who in America* for individual achievement. Synclaire lives in Pittsburgh where she attends college. Visit her website at **bonniesynclaire.com**.